A CARPENTER CALLED JOSEPH

KENNETH A. WINTER

WildernessLessons

JOIN MY READERS' GROUP FOR UPDATES AND FUTURE RELEASES

Please join my Readers' Group so i can send you a free book, as well as updates and information about future releases, etc.

See the back of the book for details on how to sign up.

A Carpenter Called Joseph

"The Called" - Book 1 (a series of novellas)

Published by:

Kenneth A. Winter

WildernessLessons, LLC

Richmond, Virginia

United States of America

kenwinter.org

wildernesslessons.com

Edited by Sheryl Martin Hash

Cover design by Scott Campbell

ISBN 978-1-7367155-3-6 (soft cover)

ISBN 978-1-7367155-4-3 (e-book)

ISBN 978-1-7367155-5-0 (large print)

Library of Congress Control Number: 2021913759

DEDICATION

In memory of my dad,
Bob Winter,
a gifted woodworker and a loving father

who loved his wife, his kids, his grandkids, and his great grandkids well,

but, most importantly, he pointed us all to Jesus,
the One whom he faithfully followed.

∾

The Lord your God cared for you all along the way
… just as a father cares for his child.
(Deuteronomy 1:31)

∾

CONTENTS

FROM THE AUTHOR

A word of explanation for those of you who are new to my writing.

You will notice that whenever i use the pronoun "I" referring to myself, i have chosen to use a lowercase "i." This only applies to me personally (in the Preface). i do not impose my personal conviction on any of the characters in this book. It is not a typographical error. i know this is contrary to proper English grammar and accepted editorial style guides. i drive editors (and "spell check") crazy by doing this. But years ago, the Lord convicted me – personally – that in all things i must decrease and He must increase.

And as a way of continuing personal reminder, from that day forward, i have chosen to use a lowercase "i" whenever referring to myself. Because of the same conviction, i use a capital letter for any pronoun referring to God throughout the entire book. The style guide for the New Living Translation (NLT) does not share that conviction. However, you will see that i have intentionally made that slight revision and capitalized any pronoun referring to God in my quotations of Scripture from the NLT. If i have violated any style guides as a result, please accept my apology, but i must honor this conviction.

Lastly, regarding this matter – this is a <u>personal</u> conviction – and i share it only so you will understand why i have chosen to deviate from normal editorial practice. i am in no way suggesting or endeavoring to have anyone else subscribe to my conviction. Thanks for your understanding.

∾

PREFACE

~

This novella is a fictional work about the life of Joseph, the carpenter. No other man in history has been charged with the tremendous responsibility he was given. He was ordained by the Almighty God to be the earthly father to His one and only Son. That statement alone tells us volumes about the character of Joseph. He wasn't randomly chosen by God. He wasn't chosen simply because he and Mary were engaged to be married. He and Mary were betrothed because God had chosen them both and ordered their steps accordingly … from before the beginning of time.

Imagine God's criteria for the man who would raise His Son through childhood, adolescence, and early adulthood. Imagine the character and heart the Father would require Jesus's earthly father to possess. We often talk about Proverbs 31 being a gold standard for women. i suggest that Joseph is the Matthew 1 gold standard for men. We only read about a few of his character traits in the chapter. Matthew writes: He was a "just" man. He was a "considerate" man. He was faithful to do what God directed him to do.

But i believe the most important aspect of his character is not specifically mentioned; it's inferred. He was a man after God's own heart! How is it that i can say that with conviction? Simple! Who else do you think the Almighty God would entrust to father His Son?

Through this story we'll explore the heart and character of Joseph as presented in the Gospels of Matthew and Luke. We'll also consider what that may have looked like in their day-to-day lives not recorded in Scripture. The writers of the Gospels were led by the Holy Spirit to write just what the Heavenly Father wanted us to know about Joseph and the earthly family of Jesus. There were many details left unwritten. Those details prompt questions. We will not know the answers to many of those questions until we stand before our Lord. And by then, we may no longer care.

But the purpose of this work is to imagine some of those details and questions. Let me hurriedly point out that not one of those details changes the narrative of the Gospels one jot or tittle. i have taken great care in the writing of this work to guard the sanctity and truth of the Gospel message. i am not attempting to add to those truths. Rather, my goal is to prompt you to consider the truths as recorded in Scripture. My additions are purely for your reading entertainment as you do so.

The story is written in first person with Joseph as the storyteller. Toward the end, his son, James, adds his voice, as he tells a portion of the story as well. My hope is that you draw your chair up close and listen, not just to the story, but to what i believe was in their hearts as they share their very personal reflections about Jesus.

Most of the other characters in the story also come directly from Scripture. You will easily recognize them. However, where the Bible is silent, i have chosen to add background details about many of the people, just like i have Joseph and James, which are either purely fictional or assumptions not confirmed in Scripture. These background details are added to further the telling of the story.

Some of the characters are seen in Scripture – but not necessarily tied to the birth and early life of Jesus. Their inclusion in this work is either conjecture or complete fiction. But i have included them because of the unique perspective they bring to the story.

Lastly, several of the characters are totally fiction. For example, i do not believe Joseph attempted to find a room in Bethlehem at the first century "Holiday Inn." i believe he intended to stay with family. So, a few of the fictional characters are his extended family members whom i have created to receive them. You will not find them in Scripture!

Like my novels and short story collections, you will also encounter fictional twists and turns that are an attempt to fill in the blanks where Scripture is silent regarding certain day-to-day events. Again, my prayer is that nothing in the story detracts from scriptural truth; rather, while remaining true to the biblical story, it tells it in a way that creates an interesting and thought-provoking reading experience.

Throughout the story, some instances of dialogue are direct quotes from Scripture. Whenever i am quoting Scripture, you will find that it has been italicized. The Scripture references are included in the back of this book. Those remaining instances of dialogue not italicized are a part of the fictional stories to help advance the storyline. However, i have endeavored to use Scripture as the basis in forming any added dialogue by a historical character with the intent that it does not detract from the overall message of God's Word.

My prayer is, that as you read this story, you will see Joseph and his entire family through new eyes – and more importantly, that you will be challenged to see Jesus through their eyes.

~

1

MY FRIENDSHIP WITH ELI

∽

J am a carpenter named Joseph. My father, Jacob, was also a carpenter, as was his father, Matthan. As a matter of fact, my ancestors have been carpenters as far back as anyone can remember. Well, maybe not as far back as *anyone* remembers. My ancestor David was actually a shepherd – until he became the King of Israel. And his son Solomon is considered by many to have been the wisest king our people ever had.

Thirteen of my ancestors, who came after Solomon, followed him in ruling over our nation as kings of Judah. Most of them did evil in the eyes of the Lord – so I share my family connection with them with great reluctance. But there is no denying that royal blood courses through my veins.

We are God's chosen people living in the land He promised our patriarch, Abraham, about 2,000 years ago. But though we live in the land God gave us, we have been living here as subjects under foreign rulers for over 500 of those years. Our people have been subjected to the rule of the Babylonians, the Persians, the Greeks, the Seleucids, and now the Romans.

· · ·

We have long grown weary under pagan rulers who have little regard for our Lord God Jehovah. We pray for deliverance from our oppression much like our ancestors prayed for their deliverance from Egyptian bondage.

Our God promised, through the prophets, to send His Messiah to deliver us. Each generation for hundreds of years has hoped and believed He would come in their lifetime. But 400 years have passed since the last great prophet, Malachi – and all we have heard from heaven is silence! Our hearts are heavy, and our hope has grown dim, but we live our lives trusting our God for His promise.

Since my ancestor King David grew up in and around the town of Bethlehem, it is considered my family home. Some of my relatives still live there. But over the centuries, much of my family has scattered to other parts of Judea and Galilee.

My great-great-grandfather, Eliud, led his family to settle in the city of Cana. The town was destroyed by the Assyrians many years before, but Eliud and others went there to rebuild it. His carpentry skills were put to great use as the town rose from its ashes.

And the generations of my family that followed him also assisted in that effort. As a matter of fact, my younger brother, Clopas, and I made a steady living there with our carpentry skills for quite a while. But when work began to slow down in Cana, I learned there was more opportunity in nearby Nazareth. Clopas decided to remain in Cana, while my wife, Rebekah, and I moved to Nazareth.

Soon after I arrived in Nazareth, I met a carpenter named Eli. He needed a partner and I needed steady work – so we agreed that Jehovah God had brought us together. Eli and his wife, Abigail, soon became good friends to Rebekah and me.

I remember the day Abigail gave birth to a baby girl they named Mary. She was the apple of Eli's eye and he doted on her from the day she was born.

Eli would occasionally bring her to work with him when she was a little girl. I watched her grow from a tiny infant into a tender young woman.

Mary always had a soft and gentle nature. She honored her parents in all she did and exhibited a great love and reverence for our God. She was a hard worker and had a quick wit.

Abigail died when Mary was nine, and I will never forget the tenderness she showed Eli as he walked through the grief of losing his wife – despite the fact Mary was walking through her own.

Then, not long afterward, my Rebekah died. She had developed a high fever that the rabbi and midwife were unable to cure. Eli and Mary were both a great comfort to me during my time of grief.

Rebekah and I had been married for twenty years before she died. Early in our marriage we came to realize Rebekah could not have children. Though it was a source of great sadness throughout our marriage, we had come to trust that it was the will of God. Still, I always regretted not having a son to mentor.

A few years after Rebekah's death, I started wondering, and praying, if God would give me an opportunity to marry again and give me a son. But I never anticipated how God would answer that prayer!

~

THE BETROTHAL AND A SENSE OF BETRAYAL

∽

*E*li and I watched as Mary continued to mature into a radiant young woman. She caught the attention of all the young men in our town. So, no one was more surprised than I when Eli approached me one evening after we had finished our work.

"Joseph, come, sit a moment," he said. "I have something I wish to discuss with you."

"Of course, my friend," I replied. "I saw you speaking with the rabbi earlier today. Does he have some work he would like us to do? We need a longer term project than those we've been working on as of late."

"Yes, this is most definitely longer term," he responded with a bit of a twinkle in his eye. But it's not a work project I'm considering."

"What is it?" I asked.

. . .

"I'd like you to consider marrying my daughter!" he declared.

I was speechless! Since I am only slightly younger than Eli, I am old enough to be Mary's father. Though such an age difference is not uncommon in marriages of our day, it still was not a match I had considered. However, I admit the possibility was captivating. I told Eli I would pray about his offer.

Over the next several days I made a rather lengthy mental list of all the reasons why I was not the right man for Mary. But I could not think of one single reason why she would be unsuitable for me. As I prayed, I sensed God was leading me to go back to Eli.

"I would be honored and humbled to take your daughter Mary as my wife," I told Eli. "I am grateful for your trust in me that I would care and provide for her. You know I would love her with my whole heart."

"Wonderful!" Eli exclaimed. "I know you will. We will begin making arrangements for your wedding this very day and ..."

I interrupted him, "Not so fast, my friend. Before I can give you my final answer, I must know that this is what Mary wants, as well. I will not enter into a marriage arrangement that she does not desire. So, you need to discuss the matter with her and let me know what she says."

Truth be told, I thought it would be the last time he and I ever spoke of it. I was certain Mary had her heart set on a different match. So, I was shocked when he returned a week later to tell me Mary was also in favor of our betrothal. She was willing to become my wife!

It was all I could do to keep from shouting with delight – and thanking God for His goodness! Of all men, I was the most envied when three weeks later we announced our betrothal. We set a date for the wedding feast to be held one year later.

. . .

Soon after our announcement, Mary unexpectedly traveled to Hebron to visit her cousin for three months. When she returned, she came to Eli and me with startling news.

"Abba … and Joseph," she said as she looked at both of us in the eyes. "I'm pregnant!"

Eli and I stood there in shock and simply looked at each other. But Mary wasn't finished with her news. She assured us she was still a virgin. She told us she had become pregnant by the Holy Spirit.

"An angel by the name of Gabriel appeared to me," Mary explained. "He told me that God has decided to bless me! He said I would become pregnant and have a son. He will be very great, and He will be called the Son of the Most High God. The Lord God will give Him the throne of David. And He will reign over Israel forever. His kingdom will never end.

"I asked the angel how this could be possible, and he told me the Holy Spirit would come upon me, and the power of the Most High God would overshadow me."

She saw the heartbroken expression on my face and Eli's look of despondence.

She continued, "Joseph, I have not broken our vows. This is an act of our Most High God. I do not fully understand what is happening – but I know I must trust Him. And I need to know that you trust me. Do you believe all I have told you is true?"

My heart was broken! I hadn't really heard much else after she said the word pregnant. She said something about the Holy Spirit coming upon her. But all I could think about was this young woman, whom I thought was without guile, had somehow sullied herself and broken our contract.

· · ·

I thought about the shame and disgrace to which she and my dear friend, Eli, would be subjected. I thought about the hushed conversations that would occur behind my back.

Without saying a word, Eli got up from his seat and walked out of his home. I didn't know what else to do, so I did the same thing. My heart was full, and at that moment I could not speak.

As I made my way back home, I kept going over what Mary had said. I had gone from having a heart overflowing with joy to having a heart that had been broken into pieces.

But as much as I hurt, my love for her did not diminish in any way. I decided the right thing to do was quietly break our betrothal so as not to disgrace her publicly. Eli could then send her away to stay with a distant relative.

∾

3

CONFIRMED BY AN ANGEL

∼

*M*y sleep that night was fitful. In the midst of it, an angel of the Lord appeared to me in a dream. *"Joseph, son of David,"* he said, *"do not be afraid to go ahead with your marriage to Mary. For the child within her has been conceived by the Holy Spirit. And she will have a son, and you are to name Him Jesus, for He will save His people from their sins.*

"All of this has happened to fulfill the Lord's message through His prophet: 'Look! The virgin will conceive a child. She will give birth to a son, and He will be called Immanuel (meaning God is with us).'"[1]

When I awoke the next morning, I ran to Eli's home. Both Eli and Mary wept as I told them what the angel had said.

"Mary," I said, "I trust all you have told me is the truth. I trust you and I trust God. How favored you are above all women! And how favored am I to become your husband and a father to this One who is in your womb!"

• • •

I was delighted to learn that God had led Eli to the same realization. Though we rejoiced in the news, we also knew what people in our town would say. Mary, most of all, would be ridiculed and falsely accused of improper behavior. We trusted God would give her – and all of us – the strength we needed to endure.

Mary came home with me that day to be my wife, but she remained a virgin until after the baby was born.

Nazareth is a small town, so I knew the news about Mary would spread quickly. Eli and I decided the best thing for us to do was go talk to Jacob, our rabbi. Eli, Mary, and I would tell him about all that had happened. The rabbi would know how best to explain it to our neighbors.

When we arrived at the synagogue, Jacob was acting very strangely toward us. He had always been cordial and engaging, but today he was stern and distant. We had already decided Eli would be the first to speak.

"Rabbi, thank you for meeting with us," Eli began. "Certain events have unfolded very quickly for our family, and we have only recently become aware of some very good news."

"What is this good news?" Jacob asked.

"We want you and all of our neighbors to rejoice with us," Eli continued. "So, please allow us to tell you what has occurred. Mary will speak first."

But before Mary could say a word, Jacob interrupted, "Mary, before you speak, I want to remind you all it is my duty as the spiritual leader of this village to know every detail of what has happened so the reputation of this synagogue and our village is in no way tarnished."

"Of course, Rabbi," Eli interjected.

• • •

The rabbi continued, "I have been told that Mary is more than three months pregnant, so events have not unfolded all *that* quickly. I need to determine if anything has occurred that dishonors God or the people of this village. If anything untoward has happened, we will then discuss appropriate action.

"Mary, I have been told you have just returned from a three-month visit with your cousin, Elizabeth, in Hebron. And, as the entire village can see, you are expecting a child. I caution you to be very careful that you speak only the truth to me."

"The day before I departed for Hebron," Mary began, "I was out walking alone in the vineyard when I was approached by one whom I now know to be an angel of the Lord by the name of Gabriel.

"The angel told me, 'You have found favor with God! You will conceive and give birth to a son. The Holy Spirit will come upon you, and the power of the Most High will overshadow you. The baby will be holy, and He will be the Son of God.'"

Mary then went on to tell the rabbi how the angel told her about her cousin becoming pregnant and relayed the story of how this same angel had spoken to Elizabeth's husband, the priest, Zechariah. The angel said the priest's son would be a messenger preparing the way for the baby in her womb.

I confirmed to the rabbi that Mary and I have not consummated our marriage. She is – and will remain – a virgin until after the baby is born. Then I told him how the same angel had come to me in a dream.

"Oh?" Jacob asked. "And what did this angel of yours say?"

I replied, "The angel told me the child in Mary's womb had been conceived by the Holy Spirit. I was not to be fearful about proceeding with my marriage to Mary. He told me all of this was to fulfill the prophecy of the prophet Isaiah, 'The virgin will conceive a child.'"

Eli spoke up, saying, "God has given me a peace as well that my daughter is to be the mother of the Messiah! This is joyous news! The Messiah for whom we have all waited for centuries will soon arrive! Yes, He is even here with us right now – in the womb of my daughter!"

We all looked at the rabbi with anticipation. We were expecting him to join with us in our celebration. We were earnestly awaiting his thoughts on how we should assemble the entire town to announce this joyous news!

∾

4

THE RABBI'S REACTION

~

*A*fter a few moments of silence, Rabbi Jacob responded with a raised voice. "I directed you to tell me the truth and all you have told me are these wild stories! You tell me of an angel coming to you, Mary, in a vineyard, and you, Joseph, in a dream."

"Well, yes, Rabbi," I said. "Isn't it wonderful news?"

Jacob raised his voice even further. "Who are you that an angel of God would come to you? Angels have not walked on this earth for hundreds of years, but you expect me to believe that one has come no less than three times, including the visit to the old priest in the temple!

"If an angel had entered the temple, he would have appeared to the High Priest. If he had come to Nazareth, he would have appeared to me. He would not have come to uneducated people such as yourselves!"

Eli tried to interrupt, "But, Rabbi ..."

. . .

"Your story is preposterous!" Jacob continued. "How could a virgin conceive a child? Either you all are completely naïve or have been bewitched by this girl! Or perhaps, Joseph, you decided not to wait for a year as you announced but decided to consummate the marriage sooner. And if so, that is your prerogative if you and Eli have come to that agreement. But don't make up this wild story to cover up your impatience!"

"But, Rabbi, the prophet Isaiah wrote ...." I tried to interject.

"Do not attempt to justify your story by tying it to a questionable prophecy from Isaiah," Jacob immediately retorted. "You know our Hasmonean leaders dispute the truth of those prophecies, and they deny the belief that the Messiah will be a descendant of David."

The rabbi continued, practically shouting at us. "You have used statements no one believes to try and justify your lies! How dare you dishonor God and dishonor me by saying these things! This is blasphemy!"

Eli responded first, in a firm but unprovoked manner. "Rabbi," he implored, "we have told you the truth! The Spirit of God will confirm that truth to you if you will but seek Him in prayer – just as we have done!"

But the rabbi quickly replied, "How dare you speak to God's anointed in that way! Joseph has said he and Mary have not consummated this marriage. Either he is lying, or Mary has committed adultery with another man. The idea that the Spirit of God has come upon her is preposterous! But since there are no witnesses to indicate she has committed adultery I can only conclude the two of you have had relations – as is your right – and the baby is a product of that impetuous act!"

Mary was near tears as she said, "That is not how it happened, Rabbi."

Jacob ignored her and continued, "I will not allow you to tell your outrageous story to the people of this town! If you do, I will denounce it as heresy and call into question whether Mary is an adulteress who deserves to be stoned to death. Otherwise, we will let the people believe you have shamefully broken your commitment to a one-year betrothal period and have consummated your marriage. I will never speak a word of any of this heresy you have told me!"

The rabbi then got up and stormed out the room. As he did, he shook his robes to reflect his disdain for what we had said. As he walked away, I saw the hurt and sadness in Mary's eyes.

Our neighbors responded in much the same way. Most of them kept their distance from us, with the exception of a young neighbor girl named Salome. She was a constant source of encouragement and companionship for Mary in the weeks and months that followed. She was a friend when Mary greatly needed one.

But most everyone else we told about the angel's visits looked at us suspiciously. And others looked at us – particularly Mary – with the same disdain we had received from the rabbi. I hated that for her. God had chosen her to be His vessel. She was to be honored, not despised. But life was never going to be the same. There would always be malicious whispers uttered behind her back.

For centuries our people had waited for the arrival of the promised Messiah. I had always hoped He would come during my lifetime and that I might get a glimpse of Him. But in my wildest dreams I never thought my wife would give birth to Him. I had prayed for a son – and God had chosen me to be the earthly father of *His* Son.

All I could think about was how inadequate I was to be His father and Mary's husband. But I knew the same God who could enable a virgin to give birth to His Son would empower a lowly carpenter to be the father and husband He needed me to be. By His grace, I would trust and follow Him!

∽

5

TELLING MY FAMILY

~

I knew the next person we needed to tell was my brother Clopas, and I knew we needed to do so sooner than later. A few days after our meeting with Rabbi Jacob we set out for Cana. I prayed this conversation would go much better than the one we had with the rabbi.

Clopas is much younger than I am. Six years ago he married a young woman whose name is also Mary. We apparently share similar tastes in women since our wives have the same name! They now have a five-year-old son, James.

I last saw them three months ago while Mary was in Hebron visiting her cousin Elizabeth. They were delighted when I told them Mary and I were engaged. Though they, like everyone else, were surprised because of our age difference, they were glad to hear joy had once again returned to my heart.

The three of them had accompanied Eli and me as we traveled to Jerusalem to celebrate Passover. While we were there, we encountered our cousin Achim, who lives in Bethlehem. I had shared my joyous news with him, as well.

Clopas was surprised when Mary and I now unexpectedly showed up at his home. I explained that we had news to share with him and his family. I was amazed when I looked over at my sister-in-law. She was staring at my Mary with what appeared to be a "knowing" look.

"You look like you are bursting with excitement," Clopas exclaimed. "Tell us your important news, Joseph!"

After we were all seated, I began. "Soon after we announced our betrothal, an angel of the Lord came to Mary and told her Jehovah God had chosen her, and the Spirit of God would come over her and she would conceive a child. The child will be the Son of the Most High God. He is the Messiah – whose coming the prophets foretold."

"I'm not sure I understand what you are telling us," Clopas said.

I attempted to explain, "Isaiah wrote that the Messiah would be born of a virgin – and now God has chosen Mary to be that virgin. Mary told her father and me about the angel's visit after she returned from Hebron last month. By that time, she was three months pregnant."

Mary continued the story, saying, "The angel of the Lord told me my cousin Elizabeth was also expecting a child. My cousin is in her sixties and, to this point in her life, has been barren. Imagine my surprise! I decided I needed to go to Hebron immediately. If Elizabeth was truly pregnant, it would be confirmation that all the angel had told me was true.

"I told my father I had learned Elizabeth was pregnant, and I needed to go visit her. But I did not tell him the rest of the story. I needed to see with my own eyes before I told my father and Joseph what the angel had said. And my father was so overjoyed for Elizabeth and her husband, Zechariah, that he never inquired about the messenger.

. . .

"As I traveled to Hebron, I kept thinking about how I was going to tell my father ... and Joseph. And now, how was I going to tell Elizabeth? Would she believe me when I told her about an angel appearing to me? And would she believe what he had said?

"When I arrived at their home, I found out that Zechariah was gone. But Elizabeth greeted me. Immediately I could see she was great with child. She had the glow of an expectant mother. I was so happy for her.

"But imagine my astonishment when she cried out to me, 'God has blessed you above all women, and your child is blessed. Why am I so honored, that the mother of my Lord should visit me?'

"I didn't need to worry about what I would say to Elizabeth – she already knew! She went on to say, 'When I heard your greeting, the baby in my womb jumped for joy.'

"Any question I had about what the angel had said to me vanished! I had only been carrying the Son of God in my womb for a matter of days. There was no physical sign that I was pregnant. I had told no one about the angel or what he had said."

"But Elizabeth knew?" Clopas asked.

"She knew!" Mary answered.

"After I told her about how the angel had visited me, she told me Zechariah had been visited by an angel in the sanctuary of the temple. The angel had told him their son would be called John and he would prepare the way for the One in my womb.

. . .

"Three months later, when it was time for me to return home, I continued to ask Jehovah God how He would have me tell my father and Joseph. I knew He would show me and not abandon me."

6

A BROTHER'S ACCEPTANCE

∼

*C*lopas looked amazed as he took in everything Mary was saying. So I added, "Clopas, when Mary first told me, I didn't know what to think. But that night Jehovah God confirmed it to me through a dream. An angel told me I should bring Mary into my home as my wife. And I have done so. However, we will not consummate our marriage until after the child is born.

"You are my closest family, so we wanted you to know and understand as soon as possible. We know how shocking this all sounds. We both have experienced that same shock firsthand. So, please, feel free to ask us any questions you have."

I didn't need to wait long to hear exactly what my brother thought. "Joseph, I know you to be an upright man of integrity," Clopas responded. "I know you love God and strive to stand righteous before Him. I know you will not lie about your own actions or anyone else's. Your word and the word of Mary is all we needed to hear to know what you told us was the truth.

. . .

"We join with you in praising Jehovah God for His faithfulness in sending His Messiah, for His mercy in allowing us to now sit here in the baby's presence, and for His grace in the way He is enabling you to walk through this with Him. Mary, you truly are blessed by God above all other women. And Joseph, our God has chosen well to choose you to be the earthly father to His Son."

We all embraced and spent the rest of our time together rejoicing and praising God. Two days later, Mary and I returned home to Nazareth. God had again answered our prayer.

A few months later, we received word the Roman emperor, Caesar Augustus, had decreed that a census be taken throughout our land. We were all to return to our ancestral homes to be registered. Mary and I made preparations for the three-day journey to Bethlehem.

The baby would soon be born. This was not a good time for a trip, but we didn't have a choice. Once again, I admired Mary's bravery – not only for making such a trip during this late stage of pregnancy, but also because of the stares and whispers she would be forced to endure – particularly when we arrived in Bethlehem.

Eli had planned to travel with us since he, too, was of the line of David. But two days before we were to leave, he came down with a fever. The rabbi and midwife had seen this fever before and treated him with an elixir made from herbs and bark.

They assured Mary and me that he would recover, but he did not have the strength to travel to Bethlehem. We would go on without him and one of the midwives would look in on him during our absence.

I planned for us to stay at the home of my cousin Achim in Bethlehem. He and I had always enjoyed a close relationship, even though we lived far apart. I hoped he would welcome us with open arms.

• • •

Shortly before our departure, I received word from Clopas that he and his family would join us on the journey to Bethlehem. We were grateful to have their companionship as we traveled. They would, however, be lodging with his wife's sister when they arrived in the city.

Bethlehem is situated in the midst of rolling green hills, which produce some of the best almonds and olives throughout the province. The soil is fertile because the town sits on top of an enormous aquifer. As a matter of fact, the water from the aquifer is well known to be the best tasting water around. The story goes that some of King David's mighty men risked their lives by crossing through Philistine lines to get him a cup of that very water.

Bethlehem was once one of the fortress towns established by King David's grandson, Rehoboam. It was a defensive military installation designed to safeguard the water source, which also supplied Jerusalem and other surrounding villages. But now under Roman rule, it had become less of a fortress and more of a sleepy village secluded from the fervent pace and activity of Jerusalem.

The hills in and around Bethlehem are ideal for raising sheep. The rich soil and plentiful water provide an abundant food supply. The demand for sacrificial lambs in Jerusalem continues to grow. They are the principal animal sacrifice offered in the temple throughout the year.

And during the feasting days, Jerusalem is filled with pilgrims from all over the land who aren't able to bring their own animals to sacrifice. The pilgrims rely on the lambs and birds available at the temple. That creates great demand – and profit – for the Bethlehem shepherds.

∽

7

A JOURNEY TO BETHLEHEM

~

*W*e passed by Jerusalem on our way to Bethlehem. Even though this was not one of the feasting days, the city was still bustling with activity. Achim is a carpenter, and since there's not a lot of work for carpenters in Bethlehem, most days he works in Jerusalem. He can work there but still be home most nights, sleeping in his own bed and enjoying his wife's good cooking.

He and his wife, Miriam, have three grown sons who are also carpenters. Each of them is married, and Jehovah God has blessed them all with children – which means Miriam and Achim have been blessed with many grandchildren.

Achim has often reminded me that our ancestor King Solomon once wrote that *"children are a gift from the Lord"* and *"happy is the man whose quiver is full of them."*[2] God continues to enlarge my cousin's quiver!

Each time I visit Achim, his house is bigger. All his family lives under one roof, so every time a son marries or has children, Achim simply adds another room. Like most of the homes in Bethlehem, his is made of stone with wood timber beams to support the upper floors. The house also abuts a hill, so the stable for the animals is actually a cave Achim enlarged within the hill.

Several years ago, Achim added a third level to his home. The center courtyard is open to allow for cooking, eating, and gathering. That is where they spend most of their time together. The other rooms either surround or overlook the courtyard. Those rooms provide adequate space for sleeping and privacy. When I last saw him, he told me he had added extra rooms to provide space for guests.

Achim and Miriam have graciously invited our extended family to stay with them or with other family members who also live in Bethlehem. As the patriarch of our extended family there in Bethlehem, Achim has made sure space is available for the entire family.

In fact, he sent word that he has reserved a room in his home just for me! I had shared with him earlier the good news about Mary and me. He and Miriam were genuinely pleased. They knew how devastated I was after losing Rebekah.

They had been planning to travel to Nazareth to join in the celebration of our wedding feast the following spring. But now there would be no wedding feast. They didn't yet know Mary would be arriving with me.

Achim appeared in the doorway to greet me before I even had a chance to knock on their door. His arms were outstretched, his eyes twinkled, and his smile extended from one ear to the other.

In his usual gregarious fashion, Achim called out, "Welcome, Joseph! We have been watching for your arrival! We are so happy ..."

Suddenly, he stopped in mid-sentence and pulled away from our embrace, staring over my shoulder at Mary. At that same moment, Miriam arrived at his side. She, too, was wearing a big smile that only broadened when she saw Mary.

"You are radiant, my dear!" Miriam declared. "And you must be weary from your journey. Come in, come in! We won't have you standing there in the doorway!"

But just as Miriam went to embrace Mary and usher us into their home, Achim placed his hand on Miriam's shoulder to stop her. The two of them exchanged disapproving looks. Suddenly there was an awkward silence.

Finally, I said, "Achim and Miriam, this is Mary, my wife."

The two looked at me, then at Mary – followed by a not-so-subtle stare at her obvious "baby bump." The silence became even more awkward.

"I know you must have questions," I continued. "But may we come in so Mary can sit and rest, and we will explain everything that has occurred?"

Miriam nodded her head in agreement and reached out a hand to help Mary across the threshold. But Achim continued to block the doorway and removed Miriam's hand from Mary's shoulder.

∼

8

"THERE IS NO ROOM FOR YOU!"

~

This time Achim broke the silence saying, "Yes, I do have questions, Joseph, and they must be answered before you can enter my home. When is the child she is carrying due?"

"Any day now," I replied.

I obviously knew what he was about to ask next.

"Joseph, when we last saw you, you said you were engaged to this young woman and the marriage feast was still nine months away. That was only a little more than six months ago. How can she now be expecting a baby any day, and how is it she has become your wife well in advance of your wedding feast?"

I had hoped to tell them all that had transpired sitting in the comfort of their home. I wanted Mary to be able to sit down and rest. But that was not an option since Achim would not budge from their doorway.

· · ·

So, I explained how Mary had been visited by an angel who told her the Spirit of God would come upon her, and she would give birth to His Son. Then I told them how the angel had subsequently appeared to me and told me the same thing. As a result, we had gone ahead and formalized our marriage contract right then, and I had brought Mary into my home.

"But she is still a virgin as the prophets foretold," I added. "And we will not consummate our relationship until after the baby is born."

Achim's demeanor showed no signs of softening. He was staring at me with a disgusted look on his face, and I knew his reaction was going to be very different from Clopas's.

"Either she is a liar," he accused, "and you are so lovestruck you have been blinded to her deception. Or you are both liars and have made up this unbelievable story to cover up her adultery.

"If the baby is yours, why have you said you have not yet consummated your marriage? Whoever heard of Jehovah God coming upon any woman to give birth to a baby? Babies are only conceived one way – and it requires a woman and a *man*!"

"Yes, Achim," I said in an attempt to help him understand, "but the message of the angel…."

But he was not going to allow me to interrupt him. He continued, "And whoever heard of angels appearing to anyone? Of course, there are stories in our Scripture about how angels appeared to the patriarchs, but that was a long time ago. That doesn't happen anymore!"

Achim was seething with rage.

He continued, "This is most obviously a violation of God's command-ments, and I will not accept it. I cannot allow you into my home because I would be lending credence to this outrageous story and violating every-thing I believe to be righteous and holy! You are my relative, and until now I have considered you to be my dear friend. But the two of you stand before me as an abomination before God, expecting to enter my home as if everything is all right.

"There is no room for you in my home or in the homes of any of our family members! I will see to it you are not welcome in any home in Beth-lehem! There is no room for you! You have sinned against God, and you have stained our family name."

Then he turned his back to us and shouted, "Go away from my home!"

I saw the hurt in Mary's eyes. I had hoped Achim would realize we were telling the truth, rejoice with us in the news, and embrace us like my brother had. But instead, he unleashed his wrath on us. The baby would be born any day now, and I had no idea where we were to go. I silently began to pray to God.

Almost immediately, Miriam spoke up. "You can spend the night in our stable. It will provide shelter, and the animals will provide warmth from the cool night air. There is straw to provide you with a comfortable resting place, and I will bring you food and water for the night."

As she spoke, Achim turned to silence her, but she gave him a look that left no doubt it was his turn to be silent.

"Thank you for your kindness," Mary said quietly.

The two of us followed Miriam to the stable, and I thanked God for His provision. As the sun began to set, we could hear other distant family members as they arrived and were welcomed into the home. On two occa-sions, Achim led the animals of his other arriving guests into the stable. But he did not speak a word to us, and other than Miriam, we saw no one else.

. . .

Miriam brought us food, water, and blankets. She took great care to make sure Mary was as comfortable as possible given the circumstances. We knew she did not agree with Achim's actions, but to her credit, she never spoke a word against him.

～

9

THE BABY IS BORN

~

*L*ater that night, Mary went into labor. Neither of us had any experience about what to do, and there were no family members to help her. Miriam was the only one besides Achim who even knew we were here. There was no time to send word to Clopas and his wife or send for a midwife.

Mary was calmer than I was. She told me what to do, and I tried to help her get as comfortable as possible. Beyond that, I prayed to Jehovah God!

I knew God had chosen my wife to bear His Son. I knew she was blessed above all women. But I had never admired her as much as I did at that moment. She showed incredible strength and courage. She may have gotten pregnant without human effort, but I can assure you the birth of Jesus required plenty!

Mary was in labor for several hours. Even though she was giving birth to God's Son, the painful ordeal of childbirth that resulted from Eve's sin in the Garden of Eden was not lessened for my wife. But Mary endured it all!

. . .

Later she told me, "When I heard Jesus cry out for the very first time, all the pain was worth it. As the Son of God, He will always be my God; but as the Son of Man, He will always be my baby boy. I have loved my God as His child for as long as I can remember, but now I will love His Son with a mother's never-ending love."

We knew Jesus was the Son of God, and we knew God had sent Him to this earth. But we didn't completely know why He had come. We didn't know what He would do or what He would endure. But at that moment, as Mary fed Him for the first time, I looked at them both and marveled at this precious gift from God.

Even the animals in the stable seemed to be in awe. Not one of them made a sound. It was as if they realized they were in the presence of their Creator.

We basked in that special moment as we both held Him in our arms for the next hour or so. I added fresh straw to one of the animal feeding troughs, then covered it with one of the clean blankets Miriam had provided for us. Mary had already wrapped Jesus in the swaddling clothes she had brought for that purpose.

As I laid Him in that manger, Mary began to sing the song I had heard her sing many times before:

"With all my heart, I praise the Lord, and I am glad because of God my Savior. He cares for me, His humble servant. From now on, all people will say God has blessed me. God All-Powerful has done great things for me, and His name is holy. He always shows mercy to everyone who worships Him. The Lord made this promise to our ancestors, to Abraham and his family forever!" [3]

As we looked at Jesus sleeping in the manger, the message of that heart song became even more real to us both. After a while, the stillness of the night was broken. At first, we heard the shuffling sound of feet just outside the stable. It was too late at night for guests to be arriving at Achim's home. We knew it couldn't be Miriam or Achim coming to check on us. Who was it?

Just then, I saw a young boy peer hesitantly into the stable. He was immediately followed by a man who stopped and gently put his hand on the boy's shoulder. Soon I saw several more men standing behind them. I could tell they were shepherds.

The young boy was the first to step inside the stable. He was staring at Jesus lying in the manger and slowly began to approach Him. The others followed, with heads bowed. I knew they had not come to do us any harm.

The shepherd boy stopped and looked at Mary. It was obvious he was seeking permission to come closer to Jesus to get a better view. Mary never hesitated. She smiled and nodded her head for the boy to approach. Then he looked at me, and I did the same. It was as if he and the other shepherds already knew who the baby was.

~

10

THE SHEPHERDS COME TO WORSHIP

∿

One by one, first the boy, then the men began to kneel in front of the manger. The one who appeared to be the boy's father said, "My name is Moshe. This is my son, Shimon. We, together with these other men, are shepherds. Two nights ago, my wife gave birth to my third son. I don't think she and I would have been as welcoming to strangers inter- rupting this private moment as you two are being to us. Please allow me to explain the reason for our intrusion.

"Tonight we were watching over our flocks in the hills overlooking the town. It has been a clear still night without a cloud in the sky. The sheep were contented, so it was a quiet night in the hills. And as we looked down on the town, it, too, was still.

"Shimon was excitedly telling me how he and his younger brother, Jacob, were going to help me train up their new baby brother to be a good shep- herd. When suddenly, our tranquility was interrupted by the appearance of what looked to be a man – but a man unlike any I have ever seen. He was surrounded by a blinding light.

· · ·

"While I raised a hand to shield my eyes, I instinctively reached out to pull Shimon close to my side. I squinted at the other shepherds who were near. We all were trying to discern what was happening and what we should do. Did this man mean us harm? Should we run? But we all knew we could not abandon our sheep! Who was this man and what did he want? Instead of feeling threatened, the light seemed to embrace us. Don't misunderstand – we were afraid! But at the same time, we were spellbound.

"*'Don't be afraid!'* the man said. *'I bring you good news of great joy for everyone! The Savior – yes, the Messiah, the Lord – has been born tonight in Bethlehem, the city of David! And this is how you will recognize Him: you will find a baby lying in a manger, wrapped snugly in strips of cloth!'*[4]

"We were still trying to understand who this being was when, all of a sudden, the sky was filled with a heavenly host. As if in unison, we all fell to our knees in fear and shielded our eyes from the brilliance that radiated above us. At that point, we knew this was a host of angels – the army of heaven – who had come to bring us great news.

"The angelic host began praising God, saying: *'Glory to God in the highest heaven, and peace on earth to all whom God favors!'*[5]

"As the angels proclaimed their news, time seemed to stop. Even the sheep surrounding us seemed to bow low. No one – and no thing – was capable of moving. We were overwhelmed by the sight and enraptured by the news. I have no idea how long the angelic host remained in our midst.

"Then we did something that shepherds never do! We left our flocks unattended in the field. We didn't hesitate for one moment. We ran into town to this stable just as the angels had directed us.

"As we approached the stable, we expected to find a large crowd gathered to worship the arrival of the newborn Messiah. We thought the religious leaders would all be gathered to give praise to God – and perhaps even

King Herod himself would be here. This is a great night of rejoicing for our entire nation in celebration and worship. Glory to God in the highest!

"But we are dumbfounded that no one is here. Not even Achim, who owns this stable, or his family. At first we thought, surely this isn't the place! And yet, we know it is! Why are we seemingly the only ones who know who this baby is?"

He hadn't really directed that question to us; rather, he was making an observation. Moshe and the others turned their attention back toward Jesus and worshiped Him. Neither Mary nor I knew how to respond. Instead, Mary gave them a tender smile and nodded her head in acknowledgment.

After a while, they quietly stood to their feet and reverently backed out of the stable. The boy was the last to get up. I could see he was staring into Jesus's eyes. He apparently had discovered what Mary and I had seen earlier.

Jesus's eyes are inviting and gentle. They welcome you in and make you feel safe. But they also seem to look into your very soul. Even though newborns are not supposed to be able to focus, Jesus is able to do just that!

After a few moments, Moshe softly called out to his son, "Shimon, it's time to go."

∿

11

OUR FAMILY IS SEPARATED

~

$\mathcal{T}$he shepherds were not as quiet leaving the stable as they had been arriving. We could hear their excitement as they shared everything they had seen, heard, and experienced. But no one else came to visit us that night except Miriam.

She had evidently heard the shepherds when they arrived. I caught a glimpse of her in the shadows standing just outside the stable but still within earshot of what was being said. When the shepherds left, she returned to the house.

A few hours later, but still well before sunrise, she and Achim came into the stable. They walked directly to the manger. As Miriam looked down at Jesus, I could see her countenance softening. Achim's expression, however, remained unchanged. Miriam turned toward Mary.

She said, "Your baby is beautiful, my dear. What is His name?"

Mary answered, "His name is Jesus – just as the angel instructed us."

. . .

"And how are you feeling?" Miriam continued.

"Jehovah God has been gracious and faithful!" Mary replied. "He gave me the strength I needed and the courage to endure throughout the birth – just as He did in the days leading up to the birth. He has blessed me with a husband who seeks to honor Him as well as honor me. He, too, has been my strength and courage throughout it all.

"Now God has blessed us with this beautiful baby – to love, to care for, and to raise. I am truly blessed above all women! And we thank you for your kindness in providing us with this place for me to give birth to my baby."

"That is why we have come to see you this morning," Miriam responded. "Achim and I can no longer allow you and your baby to remain in this animal stable."

I silently lifted up a prayer. "God, where would You have us go now?"

"We have decided you must move into the room we had prepared for Joseph inside the house," she continued. "It is on the upper floor away from the rest of the family. You will have a comfortable bed and a warm place for your baby. I will provide you with all you need each day.

"It will be a place for you to rest and regain your strength until your forty days of purification are completed. But no one in the house is to know you are there, and you are not to venture out of the room. We all must be agreed on this condition."

"What will the others think when they hear the cries of a baby coming from the room?" Mary asked.

. . .

"We have twelve grandchildren living in our home, a number of whom are crying babies, so no one will be able to distinguish the sounds of one more," Miriam replied. "And the room in which you will be staying is far removed from the others, so that should not be an issue."

But something told me there was something else – and I didn't need to wait long to discover what it was. As I looked at Achim, I could clearly see this was not his idea; but apparently Miriam had prevailed. Achim turned to me and said, "Joseph, there is one condition to this arrangement. You will not be permitted to stay in our home with Mary and the baby. I cannot turn a blind eye to your sinful behavior. You may return on the baby's eighth day for His circumcision and on His fortieth day to retrieve them. Otherwise, you must stay away.

"It is best you leave Bethlehem during this time. There is plenty of work in Jerusalem for a capable carpenter. And I am sure you will be able to find a room in the city where you can stay. The sun will rise soon. We need to move Mary and the baby into the house before the rest of the family awakens. And Joseph, you need to leave now, as well."

I hated to leave Mary and Jesus, but I knew Miriam would take good care of them. Mary looked at me and reluctantly nodded her agreement, but I could see how unhappy she was with this arrangement. The joy we had shared with a group of unknown shepherds over the birth of Jesus was now being overshadowed by the doubts of our own family.

I embraced my wife, saying, "Jehovah God has been faithful in ordering every step that has led us here, and we will trust Him, knowing He will continue to do so."

Turning to my cousin I said, "Thank you, Achim, for allowing Mary and Jesus to stay in your home, and thank you for the care I know you will provide them."

Achim nodded curtly. Miriam ushered Mary and Jesus into the house, and I set out for Jerusalem.

12

MY FIRST WEEK IN JERUSALEM

~

*B*efore I could leave Bethlehem, there were two things I needed to do. First, I went to the synagogue as soon as the doors opened and registered for the census. Then, I sought out Clopas at his sister-in-law's home. I told him what had occurred since we arrived the day before.

I told him Jesus had been born and how a group of angels had announced His birth to shepherds in the hills. I told him how the shepherds had come to worship Jesus. I told him the joys, the wonders, and the awe of everything that had transpired.

"But Achim does not believe any of this is true," I continued. "He does not believe Jesus is the Son of God. He believes that either Mary committed adultery, or she and I violated our betrothal agreement and consummated our marriage before the proper time. He refused us entry into his home, but Miriam prevailed upon him to allow us to spend the night in their stable.

"Now that Jesus has been born, he has agreed to allow Mary and the baby to stay in the house until her time of purification is complete. However, I am not welcome in their home. I am headed to Jerusalem to find work for the next few weeks until Mary's time is completed."

"Brother, I am so sorry Achim has treated you this way," Clopas replied. "I would see if you could stay here in this home, but I know they have no room."

"That is very kind of you, brother," I responded. "I know Jehovah God has a divine plan in all of this. So we will trust Him that He will use this to further His purpose in all our lives.

"I have come to ask a favor of you. It will be several weeks before Mary and I can return to Nazareth. Would you please stop in Nazareth on your way home to Cana and check on Eli? Tell him Jesus has been born, and we will return as soon as we can."

Without hesitation, Clopas replied, "We most definitely will do so! Is there anything else we can do for Mary and the baby while you are in Jerusalem?"

"No, thank you!" I answered. "Since they are staying in the home secretly, they will not be able to receive you. I am, however, confident Miriam will take good care of them."

I bid my brother farewell and set out for Jerusalem. It quickly became apparent that Achim had been correct about there being plenty of work in the city! Renovations were being made to Herod's palace, and I was hired to help with the work that very afternoon.

Over the years, most of the merchants in the city have added rooms over their shops to accommodate the many pilgrims who come to Jerusalem for the annual feasts. It did not take me long to find a place to stay for the next forty days.

. . .

My days were very predictable. Six days per week I arose at the sound of the cock's crow and worked until the evening hours. Then each evening and on the Sabbath day I went to the temple to pray and seek God's face. I prayed for the safety of my wife – and His Son.

I will confess that though I knew Jesus was God's Son, from the moment He emerged from the womb, my heart embraced Him as my own son. He is the Son of Jehovah God who entrusted me to be His earthly father. From the moment He was born, He was both my God ... and my son.

Each night I prayed for the wisdom, understanding, strength, and ability as one who is a sinner to be the father to a son who will know no sin. I prayed I would be faithful to the task to which God had called me. I knew I would never be worthy – and yet, I also knew God had chosen me.

"Heavenly Father," I prayed, "grant me the ability to be the father You would have me be – to Your Son!"

In some respects the days passed slowly. I missed my family. But in other ways, time seemed to fly. Before I knew it, Jesus was eight days old!

∾

13

THE CIRCUMCISION OF JESUS

❧

I woke up early in the morning so I could arrive at Achim's home well before the household began their day. Achim and Miriam were expecting me, so Achim met me at the door and quietly led me up to the room where Mary and Jesus were staying. Mary had been anticipating my arrival as well, and we both savored those few moments together.

Mary placed Jesus in my arms, and I quietly followed Achim back outside. The sun was just beginning to reveal itself above the horizon. I would take Jesus to the synagogue and then return with Him by mid-morning in time for His next feeding. The rabbi would not be at the synagogue for at least another hour, so I decided to walk out to the hill country on the eastern side of town.

As I looked at Jesus asleep in my arms, I could not get over how light and fragile He was. It was hard to imagine God would choose to send His Son in the form of a baby. He is the Creator of life, but He had chosen to come in the form of His creation. He is all powerful, but He has chosen to come in the form of a powerless baby.

. . .

I had never held a baby in my arms for this long. I had held my nephew when he was born, and, of course, I had held Jesus soon after He was born. However, in both cases, their mothers were nearby to rescue me if the babies began to cry. For the next few hours, I would be on my own. Truth be told, I was somewhat intimidated – not so much because Jesus was the Son of God – rather because He was a little baby!

As I walked along the hillside, Jesus opened His eyes. He looked up at me with those all-knowing eyes, as if to say, "We've got this! Don't be concerned. Let's just enjoy our time together."

An even deeper love began to swell up in my heart – a deeper love for my God and a deeper love for this little One He had entrusted into our care. I began to think about all the things I would do with Him and teach Him. Then I thought about all He would teach me!

The sun was shining brightly now, and I knew it was time to make my way to the synagogue. Jesus was to be circumcised today in accordance with the covenant God had made with our patriarch, Abraham.

There weren't many people in the streets and only a handful in the synagogue when I arrived; each of them was engaged in prayer. I approached the rabbi and introduced myself.

"Rabbi, my name is Joseph. I am from Nazareth. My wife and I came to Bethlehem to be registered for the census. Soon after we arrived, my wife gave birth. The baby is eight days old today. In accordance with our law, I have brought Him to be circumcised."

"Joseph, my name is Rabbi Levi," he replied. "It is a pleasure to meet you on this joyous occasion. But I am surprised I have not yet seen you here in the synagogue before this if you arrived over eight days ago."

"I have been working in Jerusalem while my wife completes her days of purification here in Bethlehem."

. . .

"Where is your wife staying here in town?" he asked.

"The carpenter Achim and his wife, Miriam, have kindly provided her with a room."

"They are kind people," he said, "and it is not surprising they have come to your aid. What is the child's name?"

"His name is Jesus," I said.

The rabbi responded, "That is a noble name. I will be honored to circumcise Jesus."

The rabbi recounted the covenant God had made with Abraham and that through circumcision, Jesus was entering into that covenant. I did not sense a release from the Spirit of God to enlighten him on who Jesus was and how He was a part of that covenant in more ways than one.

Jesus barely whimpered when the knife cut away His skin. I wrapped Him back up in His cloth, and we made our return journey to Achim's stable. Again, I was able to avoid contact with the few people I passed. Miriam was there waiting for us. People were now awake in the house, so I would not be able to take Him back inside to Mary. Miriam would do so. I kissed Jesus on His forehead and released Him to her care.

～

14

MY REMAINING DAYS IN JERUSALEM

⁓

*I*f I thought my first week away from Mary and Jesus was a long time, you can only imagine what the next thirty-two days were like! I was to return to Bethlehem on the fortieth day to get my wife and Jesus. We would then travel to the temple in Jerusalem to present an offering of purification on Mary's behalf and an offering of redemption for Jesus as a first-born son. We would then continue our journey back home to Nazareth.

Truth be told, Mary and I were both concerned about Eli's health. Though I knew Clopas would look in on him and attend to any immediate needs, we would feel much better once we were there and able to provide whatever continuing care he required. But I was also looking forward to being back in Nazareth as a family, living in our own home, and beginning some pattern of normalcy.

I had waited many years to have a son, and though Jesus isn't technically my son, in many ways He is. I looked forward to beginning my new role as His father.

. . .

In the meantime, I continued my routine of working from dawn to dusk six days a week and spending evenings and each Sabbath day at the temple in prayer. Herod's household manager was pleased with my work in the palace, so he had commissioned me to be a part of the team of craftsmen making needed renovations to the great meeting hall. The king was residing at his palace in Caesarea Maritima, so it was a convenient time to get this work done.

I never had reason to visit the palace in Caesarea. But I am told it rivals the handiwork of the great palaces in the world, including Rome itself. Though Caesarea has become the political capital of this region, we all know Jerusalem remains the religious and accepted capital of our land. Herod knows it as well, so periodically he travels to his Jerusalem palace to appease the religious leaders.

Having seen the remarkable improvements he commissioned to be done to the temple, I can imagine the majesty of his palace in Caesarea. The household manager assured us the same would ultimately be true of the Jerusalem palace. No expense would be spared. This king would only be satisfied with the best!

As you know I am a carpenter, but my primary building material is stone, not wood as you might have imagined. Most of the renovations being made to the palace were being done using marble. Though I had not made the journey to Bethlehem to work, a good carpenter is never without his tools.

Our work in the great hall was almost finished – not any too soon, I might add. The household manager announced to us the king would arrive in Jerusalem the next day –our final day of work. We had been working through the night to make sure the work was completed in time. I was ready to be done so I could travel to Bethlehem the following day to get my family!

The king looked over our work when he arrived and was very complimentary. He gave us permission to continue working throughout the day so we could complete the job – even though he had returned. We were surprised when the household manager entered the hall a few hours later and announced, "A royal entourage from the Parthian empire is making its way through the city in the direction of the palace. Quick! Ready the hall to receive them!"

Herod did not seem pleased by the news whatsoever! He proclaimed loud enough for all of us to hear, "I have not received any message that an envoy is coming. Who has the audacity to show up at my door without my royal permission or invitation? What matters could be so important that protocol would be so blatantly disregarded? I refuse to grant them an audience! Even the Romans extend that simple courtesy to me! I will not condescend to their breach in protocol!"

One of Herod's advisors, a scribe by the name of Annas, spoke up. "Your majesty, you know how important our trade relations are with the Parthian empire. They are also our gateway to the Han Dynasty of China. We can ill-afford to offend them. Perhaps you should at least hear what they have to say."

The silence in the room was deafening. Even the workmen did not make a sound. Finally, Herod reluctantly said, "All right! I will see them!"

～

15

AN UNEXPECTED ARRIVAL

~

The king directed the household manager to have us continue with our work. Though he had decided to receive these visitors, he was not going to treat them as honored guests. They had offended him with their unannounced arrival, and he was not going to be gracious with his reception. However, the household manager did tell us to keep our noise to a minimum as we worked.

The Parthian visitors were very flamboyant. They wore brightly colored clothing unlike anything one would see in Jerusalem, including the king's palace. They entered the hall with a great show of splendor and magnificence as they bowed regally before the king. I had never witnessed anything like it.

After they had dispensed with their initial pleasantries, the one magus, who had introduced himself as Prince Balthazar from Babylon, spoke up. "Your majesty, where is He who has been born King of the Jews? For we saw His star when it rose and have come to worship Him."

. . .

His question seized my attention. Was he referring to Jesus? How could he possibly know about His birth? As I looked at the king, I could see he had no idea to whom the prince was referring.

Herod replied, "Oh, the King of the Jews! Of course, that is why you have come! I was just preparing to address another matter before you arrived. I must go and do so, but when I return I will tell you all about the King of the Jews!"

The king then promptly exited the hall followed by his advisors. The door had not fully closed when we heard him shouting, "The King of the Jews! I am the King of the Jews! How dare they suggest that anyone apart from me has been born into those ranks! Antipas, my son, you are one of my heirs. Has news of your birth taken seventeen years to make its way to Babylon? How dare these people suggest one has been born who will displace me and my seed!"

Overhearing the king's rant, the magi looked at one another warily, realizing Herod had no idea what they were talking about. They anxiously awaited Herod's return so they could conclude their visit and continue their quest. However, an hour passed before he came back.

"Thank you for your patience while I addressed another matter of important provincial business," he announced. "Now, as to your question about One who has been born King of the Jews – our prophets foretold of One who will come – the Messiah – who will lead our people to rebel against foreign authority and return our nation to its position of glory.

"Our people have prayed for His arrival for hundreds of years. Perhaps you, yourselves, have read those writings and seek the One whose coming was foretold. When did you first observe the star in the sky?"

Balthazar replied, "About a year ago, your majesty."

· · ·

Herod nodded and said, "Yes, that is precisely when I first became aware of it, as well!"

Everyone in the hall knew he was lying. He hadn't seen a star – neither, apparently, had anyone else in his court! But he continued as if he had been earnestly seeking the baby.

He directed one of his scribes to read the prophecy aloud:

"The Christ will be born in Bethlehem of Judea, for so it is written by the prophet: 'And you, O Bethlehem, in the land of Judah, are by no means least among the rulers of Judah; for from you shall come a ruler who will shepherd My people Israel.'"

I had forgotten the prophets said He would be born in Bethlehem! God had known hundreds of years ago that Caesar would require us to travel to Bethlehem for the census. Of course, He did! Jehovah God knows it all!

My thought was interrupted when I heard Herod say, "Bethlehem! You should find the baby in Bethlehem! I had planned to go see Him myself, but I have only just arrived in Jerusalem. I have several affairs I must attend to first, so go and search diligently for the child. When you have found Him, bring me word, so that I, too, may go and worship Him."

The magi seemed pleased with his answer and promised they would return. They departed from the hall with the same pageantry with which they had arrived.

Herod seemed quite pleased with himself as he turned and addressed his advisors in a softer voice. "If these Parthian magi do, in fact, find that such a child has been born, they will return and tell me about it – and I will do what needs to be done. And if, more likely, they do not find a child, then I will be seen as magnanimous in my response to them and the Parthians foolish in their expedition. It truly is a win-win for me!"

16

THE STAR LED THEM TO ACHIM'S HOME

~

I could have told the magi and the king exactly where they would find the child! But I remained silent. What would they think if a lowly carpenter announced he knew where the Messiah had been born? And what's more, that the baby's mother was this carpenter's wife?

But I was also concerned about what Herod meant when he said he would do "what needs to be done." A chill ran down by spine. I knew I needed to get to Bethlehem to protect Mary and Jesus!

I had planned to head their way early the next morning, but now I knew I couldn't wait. Our work in the hall was nearly complete, so the household manager graciously allowed me to leave when I told him I needed to go attend to urgent family matters. He again expressed how pleased he was with my work and assured me I would be welcome to work in the palace any time.

I quickly left Jerusalem, stopping only long enough to settle the bill for my lodging. Then, I made my way in earnest to Bethlehem. When I arrived outside Achim's home, I saw a host of camels, donkeys, and servants gathered outside. Obviously, the star had led them right to Achim's door. I did not see the magi, so I surmised they were already inside the house with Mary and Jesus. I knew if I went to the doorway, I would only create a scene with Achim. I decided to watch from a distance and only attempt entry if a problem arose.

Soon I saw a child emerge from the home. It appeared to be Sarah – Achim and Miriam's granddaughter. She was beckoning some of the servants to follow her. The servants appeared to be carrying heavy boxes and chests into the home. They all remained out of my sight for quite some time.

Eventually, I saw Balthazar, together with the other magi and servants, exit the home. I watched as they mounted their animals and left. I remained hidden in the bushes – I didn't expect they would recognize me from the palace, but I didn't want to take any chances. Balthazar was speaking to his servant as they rode past me.

I heard him say, "Tonight, we have knelt before a special child. He is not just any king, but the King of all kings. The star has led us to Him. Though we must leave Him now, we must keep Him in our hearts wherever we go!"

I then heard him call out to his fellow magi, saying, "Let us camp in the hills outside Bethlehem for the night since it is late. We can return to Jerusalem in the morning and report what we have seen to King Herod."

Once again, I felt a chill run down my spine. I was afraid how Herod would respond once they brought him their report.

I turned my attention back to Achim's house. Everything was calm, and I could not see anyone stirring. I did not want to disturb the household – or Mary and Jesus – after all the excitement from the visit of the magi. I had a good vantage point right where I was, so I decided to just rest there. I would approach the house just before first light.

· · ·

My sleep, however, was interrupted by an angel. He was the same one who had told me to go ahead with my marriage to Mary. He was again speaking to me through a dream. He said, *"Get up and flee to Egypt with the Child and His mother. Stay there until I tell you to return, because Herod is going to try to kill the Child."*[6]

There was no question in my mind God had again directed me through this angel. I knew what I must do. The sun would be coming up soon. It was time for me to arise and get Mary and Jesus.

As I walked toward the house, Achim met me at the door.

~

17

SURPRISED BY MY COUSIN

To my surprise, Achim reached out and embraced me without saying a word. He lay his head on my shoulder, and I soon realized he was sobbing. His breathing was labored as he attempted to speak. Between sobs, he said, "I am ... so sorry, ... Joseph. I am sorry I did not believe you and Mary when you arrived at my home. I have always known you to walk righteously before God. And yet, ... I allowed the evil one to fill me with doubts. I have thought and spoken wicked things about you when you two were simply being faithful servants to our God.

"I refused you entry into my home! I have kept you away from your wife and the Son God has entrusted to you. I refused entry to ... the child of the Living God! I turned my back on you – and Him! God has shown me just how wrong I was! Joseph, please ... forgive me!"

I had no idea what God had done to bring him to this point, but a heavy burden had just been lifted from my heart. I, too, began to sob as I said, "I forgive you, Achim! I know what it is like to doubt the ones you love and to question the honesty of those closest to you! Mary and I also had our doubts – and questioned God – along the way. But even with your doubts, you opened your home and provided a place for Mary and Jesus to stay. I forgive you, and I thank you for caring for them these past forty days."

Achim led me to the upper room where his entire family had gathered. Those who could fit in the small space were inside the room. The rest spilled out into the hallway. Everyone was either weeping tears of joy or celebrating with words of adoration. Apparently, they had only just learned about Jesus.

In their midst, I saw my wife. She was smiling with that sweet, tender expression I had grown to cherish. I hadn't seen that smile since our brief time together right after Jesus was born. I missed that smile. I missed her. I missed Jesus.

Our eyes met and lingered for a few moments, then Mary turned her glance toward a young girl who was carefully holding Jesus. It was Sarah – the young girl I had seen last night as she led the servants into the house. Something told me she had known about Jesus long before the rest of the family.

We enjoyed this special time with our family for a short time, but I knew we needed to leave soon and travel to Egypt. I was afraid the magi were headed to Herod's palace with their report, and we would not have much time. But first we must present our offerings at the temple in Jerusalem in accordance with the laws of Moses.

"Joseph, look at the gifts a royal expedition of magi presented to Jesus!" Mary exclaimed. "They traveled from afar to see Him!"

"Yes, I saw them last night," I replied smiling, "and was in awe that Jehovah God had led them to find the King of kings! God in His infinite wisdom enabled shepherds and wise men to seek out His Son. But those whose hearts were hardened, like the religious leaders and kings, He blinded."

. . .

Achim graciously provided us with a donkey to carry the gifts the magi had given Jesus. He and his sons helped me secure the gifts, while Mary prepared herself and Jesus for the journey. Since Achim and his sons had work to do in Jerusalem, they would accompany us to the temple.

Miriam and the rest of the family bade us farewell. "We will look forward to seeing you this spring in Jerusalem for the celebration of Passover!" she said, before adding, "and what a celebration it will be!"

I smiled back and waved farewell but doubted we would be in Jerusalem in the spring.

On our way out of Bethlehem, we spotted the magi and their entourage off in the distance. They, too, had recently set out on their journey. But I was surprised to see they weren't traveling north on the road to Jerusalem. They were traveling east toward the Arabian wilderness. They would never make it to Herod's palace going in that direction. I wondered *what* had caused them to change their minds ... or, rather, *Who* had caused them to do so?

When we arrived at the temple, I saw a man staring at us. He looked familiar, but I could not immediately place him. Then it came to me – it was Rabbi Levi from Bethlehem. He was the priest who had circumcised Jesus. He was looking at all of us with great curiosity. He saw me and smiled before bowing his head in a greeting.

I began to wonder if Levi was the one religious leader God had enabled to see the arrival of His Son! Then he turned and went on his way. We bid farewell to Achim and his sons before making our way into the temple.

~

18

AT THE TEMPLE IN JERUSALEM

∽

*A*s Mary, Jesus, and I made our way through the outer courtyard of the temple, I purchased a pair of turtledoves from one of the temple merchants. We would present the turtledoves to a priest inside the temple to be placed on the altar as a purification sacrifice.

According to our laws, a woman is considered ceremonially unclean for forty days following the birth of a son or eighty days following the birth of a daughter. At the end of that time, a sacrifice is made as an atonement that she might be made ceremonially clean.

Our laws also require that if a woman's first child is a boy, he must be dedicated to the Lord. The law dates back to the night the angel of death visited all the households in Egypt, killing every firstborn son unless an animal sacrifice had been offered and the sacrifice's blood smeared on the door posts. According to the law, the firstborn son is redeemed by the giving of five shekels.

As we prepared to present our offering of redemption, I realized that this first-born Son did not need to be redeemed! God had sent this Son to redeem *us!* I wanted to shout the words throughout the temple, but God spoke to my heart telling me it was not my news to share. He would reveal His Son in His way and in His time.

We presented the turtledoves and the five shekels to the priest as required. As we turned to leave, we were approached by an elderly man who was being helped by a young boy. I instinctively raised my hand to protect my wife and child. Mary, however, reached up and lowered my hand. It was as if she knew why the man was approaching.

Tears of joy began to stream down his cheeks as he turned to Mary saying, "My name is Simeon, and this is my great-grandson, Ashriel. Almost 100 years ago, Jehovah God gave me a promise that I would see the Messiah with my own eyes before I die. I have come to this temple every day since then looking for the child. And today that promise has been fulfilled!"

He then reached to take Jesus from Mary's arms. I was surprised when she handed Him over willingly! As Simeon held Jesus, he turned his head and looked heavenward.

In a strong voice he proclaimed, *"Lord, now You are letting Your servant depart in peace, according to Your word; for my eyes have seen Your salvation that You have prepared in the presence of all peoples, a light for revelation to the Gentiles, and for glory to Your people Israel."*[7]

After a few moments, he returned Jesus to Mary's arms and spoke a word of blessing over her and me. Before he finished, an older woman came and stood in our midst. She, too, asked Mary if she could hold Jesus. Mary again graciously agreed.

As she held Jesus, she told us her name was Anna. She spoke words of praise and blessing over Jesus. I was a little startled when Mary began to tell her the story of how the angel had come to her and what he had said. She told her about the shepherds and the magi.

· · ·

For some reason, I, too, felt compelled to tell her about the vision God had given me to take my family to Egypt. I told her we were departing that very hour, as God had instructed. I added, "I do not know where we will go in Egypt, but we will walk by faith. Jehovah God has ordered our every step in the birth of His Son – and He will continue to do so!"

She abruptly asked us to wait there a minute, saying she had something she wanted to give us. When she returned, she placed a wrapped package in Mary's hands. "This is my most prized possession," she explained. "Wrap Him in this tunic, which has no seams, and use it to keep Him warm. Then one day when He becomes a Man, give it to Him and tell Him about this day."

Mary smiled at her and promised she would. As we left the temple, Mary and I marveled at how God had again enabled two very unlikely people to welcome His Son. But we also knew this would not be the last time we would marvel at – and about – Jesus.

∽

19

OUR FAMILY ARRIVES IN ALEXANDRIA

~

I had no idea where we were to go in Egypt, but I knew the Lord would show us. We set out from Jerusalem and made our way to Ashkelon on the coast of the Mediterranean Sea. From there we traveled south and west along the coast through the Sinai Peninsula.

When we reached the eastern extreme of Egypt's Nile Delta, I realized the marshes would make our travel too difficult, so we turned inland and traveled along the southern boundary of the delta until we arrived back on the coast in the city of Alexandria.

A month had passed since we left Jerusalem, and I wanted to make sure Mary and Jesus had a comfortable place to rest that night with a roof over their heads.

I had once been told that Alexandria was the largest city in the world, rivaled only by Rome. Now that we were standing in the middle of it, I easily believed that to be the case. It is a provincial capital of the Roman empire, situated on the trade route along the south side of the Mediterranean Sea, which connects Europe with the eastern empires by land and sea.

I had also heard there was a large Jewish community living in the city. As a matter of fact, I was told that Alexandria had become the largest urban Jewish community in the world, even surpassing Jerusalem. I decided the community shouldn't be too hard to find!

As we stood on the docks overlooking the sea, we were surrounded by ships of every size and nationality. Even though Mary was carrying the Son of God in her arms, we still felt very small and provincial in the midst of this vast city. We didn't know what we were to do next. So we did the only thing we knew to do. We called out to God!

"Jehovah God," I prayed, "You have directed every step we have taken in our lives. Even when we didn't know You were leading us, You have gone before us. At each turn in our journey, You have shown us where You would have us go. Please bring us someone to show us where You would have us go from here."

When Mary and I raised our bowed heads there was a young boy standing right in front of us. He smiled at us and said, "You look like you need some help! My name is Khati. How can I help you?"

I was grateful he was speaking in Aramaic!

"My name is Joseph," I replied. "This is my wife, Mary, and our son, Jesus. We are new to your city and looking for a place we can find some food and a place to rest."

"I have a little brother," Khati said, pointing at Jesus. "And he is about the same age as your baby. I can see you are Jews. Where are you from?"

. . .

"We have traveled here from Jerusalem," I answered, "but we live in the town of Nazareth."

"Someday I would like to visit Jerusalem," he responded. "I have heard many fine things about it. My family and I live in the delta quarter of our city, where many Jews live. The people there often talk about the grand temple where they say your God lives."

"Well, I wouldn't say God lives in the temple," I told him. "He lives in the hearts of His people. But the temple is a grand place for us to worship Him. We were in the temple just before we left the city! We are so very thankful for your offer to help us."

Khati smiled broadly. "My parents taught me to help others in need whenever I can. My father is a merchant, and his shop is not too far from here. I'm sure he can help you. Follow me and I will take you to him."

As we walked the few blocks to his father's shop, Khati pointed out every shop and person of interest along the way. Not only did he seem to know a lot about his city, but many of the people we passed also seemed to know him!

When we arrived at his family's shop, he introduced us to his father, Alim. He greeted us warmly, saying, "Welcome to my humble shop. You look weary from your travels. Please sit down and tell me how I can help you."

≈

20

THE FATHER'S PROVISION FOR OUR FAMILY

~

I told Alim I was looking to buy some food for my family. Then, as we continued to talk, I explained I was a carpenter looking for work and a place where we could stay. I never expected Alim's response.

"Up until last week, my cousin and his family lived in the one-room home that is adjacent to my home. At the beginning of the week, he unexpectedly announced he needed to move to another part of the city. So, for the past week, I have been looking for a new tenant. I can usually find a tenant quickly – but not this time. Perhaps it was intended for your family. I also need a good carpenter to make repairs in one of my business establishments."

As Alim went on to explain the stonework he needed done, I told him I could easily handle the job. We agreed on an exchange. Mary, Jesus, and I would move into the home he had available for the next two weeks in exchange for me completing the work he needed done.

It took me only a week to complete the work, which apparently was much quicker than he expected. "Joseph, you are a skilled carpenter," Alim said.

"Your work is far better than that of anyone else I have ever employed. And you finish the work in half the time. I will tell my friends about you, and soon you will be in great demand – and I will have a long-term tenant!"

Alim's wife, Nena, helped Mary become acclimated with the big city life of Alexandria, and the two women became fast friends. Alim's younger son was only a few months older than Jesus, so our families were quickly drawn together.

As time passed, Alim and I became good friends, as well. One day, I confided in him that we had left Judea in order to protect Jesus. I told him I had learned of a plot by Herod to massacre all the male children under two years of age born in the area where Jesus had been born. He never asked me how I learned of the plot.

I explained that we had not set out for Alexandria. We knew we were to come to Egypt, but we trusted God to direct us to the specific place He intended.

"The first patriarch of our Jewish people, Abraham," I continued, "came to Egypt over 1,900 years ago to seek refuge, just like Mary and I have done. Then Abraham's grandson, Jacob, came to Egypt over 1,700 years ago seeking refuge for his family from a famine. Our God has used Egypt in an important way in the continuing story of our people – and now even in Jesus's story."

"I am proud our people have played such an important role in your story," Alim replied. "But I also know about the years our pharaohs subjected your people to slavery. I know any kindness I extend to you and your family will never make up for the pain our pharaohs caused your people. But, perhaps it will be a small way for me to personally make amends."

Alim always avoided speaking with me about his religious beliefs. The people of Alexandria pride themselves on their acceptance and tolerance of differing beliefs. He and Nena believed in the gods of their ancestors –

the gods of the sun and the moon, and the earth and the sea. He knew that we, on the other hand, believe in the one true God who uniquely chose the Jews to be His people. Apparently, Alim's idea of tolerance and acceptance was that we would not speak of our beliefs.

However, one day all that changed. Mary told Nena about Jesus – who He is and how He came to be. She told her how she had been a virgin when she conceived. She explained how an angel had told her the Spirit of God would come upon her, and she would bear the Son of the Most High God.

In Alim and Nena's religious beliefs, stories about one of their gods impregnating a woman were not that unusual, but they had never actually spoken to a woman who had said she had been impregnated by God.

Mary even explained how the angel had spoken to Zechariah and Elizabeth, and also to me. She told Nena about the shepherds who had received an announcement from angels. And she told her about the Parthian magi who had followed a star to find Jesus.

Then she explained how an angel had told us to come to Egypt to protect Jesus. She shared with Nena how she and I believed God had directed Khati to us that very first day.

But it was the news we all received the following week that really got Alim and Nena thinking about everything Mary had said.

～

21

"WE BELIEVE!"

~

*a*lim and I were talking in his shop when Khati came rushing in. He interrupted, exclaiming, "Merchants from Jerusalem just arrived at the docks today. I overheard them talking about how the Herodian king dispatched soldiers to massacre all the male children under two years of age in and around a town called Bethlehem! I cannot believe a king would do such a thing to the children of his own people! Joseph, can this be true?"

I couldn't help but grieve over the great loss experienced by those families. God had protected His Son, but those families had paid a severe price. After a moment, I responded, "Yes, Khati, I fear that it is true."

Alim spoke up. "It is just as you said it would be, Joseph. Your God has protected your son!"

It was a few weeks before Alim approached me on the subject again, saying, "Joseph, I know you to be a man who fears your God and walks uprightly before Him. Nena and I have heard how your God has spoken to you and directed you – and how Jesus is His Son. I know you are not a devious man, and I know you believe all you have told us.

"But how is it your God would choose a young virgin from a small town, engaged to a poor carpenter, to give birth to His Son? Why wouldn't He choose a king and queen in a spectacular city like Alexandria or Jerusalem? Why would He allow His Son to be born in an animal stable and swaddled in a feeding trough instead of a majestic palace? Why would He allow kings to attempt to harm His child when they should be worshiping Him?

"Why would His angels announce the birth to a group of shepherds instead of making the announcement to people of honor and position? Why would He lead Him to be raised in a single-room hovel on the back-streets of Alexandria?"

These were questions I had wrestled with myself. And God had given me the answer. So I was grateful to now convey that answer to Alim. "Because that is what He said He would do. He said His Son would be born of a virgin. He said His Son would be born in Bethlehem. He said He would be worshiped by shepherds and foreign kings would bring tributes to Him. He said a king would slaughter children in an attempt to kill Him. He said He would direct the child to Egypt. He said He would raise a King from the line of our King David. And He said so much more!

"He said His Son would grow up in humble surroundings. And He said He will grow up to become a Man of sorrows, despised, rejected, and acquainted with the deepest grief on our behalf. He will carry our weaknesses and endure our punishment – not for His sins, but for ours."

Alim asked, "How can this be?"

"Many years ago," I continued, "Jehovah God provided a ram in a thicket to our patriarch, Abraham, to be offered as a sacrifice instead of his son Isaac. By faith, Abraham believed God would provide the sacrifice. He believed God would provide His own sacrifice on His mountain. I believe one day Jesus will be that sacrifice – the Lord will lay on Him the sins of us all. That is what I believe, and that is why I believe.

"Alim, I don't know why God chose me to be the earthly father to His Son. I have never done anything to deserve it. But I know He did choose me, and I will strive to be faithful to Him with every breath I take.

"And I don't know why He chose you to help us, but I know He did. You, too, are a part of God's plan. Each of us has a part. God is at work in and through all our lives that we might come to believe in Him and His Son. So, the question is no longer – why do I believe? The question now is – do you believe?

"When I didn't know, I asked God to show me. Are you willing – with an open heart and mind – to ask Him to show you?"

Alim remained silent. I knew he was pondering everything I had just said. I decided to give him time to consider my question, so after a few minutes I walked away.

The next morning, Alim and Nena came to our door. As I greeted him, he said, "Last night I told Nena what you said to me. When I was done, I told her, 'I believe.' And she looked at me and said, 'So do I.' Then to our surprise, Khati – who had been listening in the other room – appeared and declared, 'And so do I!' We have come to tell you we believe in your God, Jehovah, and we believe in His Son! Teach us so we can know more about Him."

From that day on, we were more than just friends – we were family! We taught them from the Scriptures and pointed them to the prophecies about Jesus.

Several weeks later, the angel again returned to me in a dream, saying, *"Get up and take the Child and His mother back to the land of Israel. Those who were trying to kill Him are dead.*[8]

I knew we could not delay. I completed my work and packed for our journey to Nazareth. Though we were glad to be returning home, we were sad to say farewell to Alim, Nena, and their family. We would miss them greatly! But we knew we would see them again one day.

〜

22

OUR JOURNEY HOME TO NAZARETH

∼

*J*ust before we left Alexandria, Mary announced she was expecting a child. I was barely able to contain my joy! This child would be flesh of my flesh. Though I knew I would never love him or her any more than I love Jesus, I rejoiced in Jehovah God's goodness in giving us this son or daughter.

Mary told me she was certain the baby was a boy. But she had no word from an angel or promise from God. This was coming simply from her own intuition. We would see how accurate that was!

Once again, I was traveling with a pregnant wife! But this time, we knew it would be several months before the baby was born. Our journey home to Nazareth would take about a month.

Jesus was now six months past His second birthday. He seemed to be enjoying the journey. He had long ago begun to walk – and it didn't take long before He was running. Now as we traveled, He was exploring every tree, every flower, and every animal we encountered along the way. He seemed to be delighting in His Heavenly Father's creation!

. . .

As I watched Him, I knew He would always be at least one step ahead of us! And yet, though He had a playful nature and a constant twinkle in His eye, He was never disobedient.

Unlike anyone else who had ever lived, Jesus was born without a sin nature. He is the Son of God, who knows no sin. That was obvious from the very beginning. He never cried for His own way. He never had a temper tantrum. He never spoke a word of disrespect or acted in any way that was disobedient.

He was also often quiet and reflective. I don't think anything ever missed His notice, and He always thoughtfully considered everything He saw and heard. From the moment He was a baby, He had the ability to look at you with those dark brown eyes as if He were looking deep into your soul. I firmly believe that even as an infant, He knew my deepest thoughts and saw me for who I truly was.

He was – and would always be – a delight to Mary and me. We marveled, simply by looking at Him. But now with another baby on the way, we began to wonder what it would be like for Him to have a younger brother or sister. How would He see Himself as He relates to them? How would they see Him?

While we were traveling home, Mary and I began to discuss what we would tell His younger brother or sister about Jesus when the child was old enough to understand.

During the conversation, Mary said, "It will be hard for His brothers or sisters to grow up with the knowledge their older brother is the Son of God. If God grants us the ability to have many more children, I want them to be close as brothers and sisters. I don't want the other children to be intimidated by Jesus or resent Him in any way. I want them to love Him as their brother – and in the proper time, as their God."

. . .

We began to pray then that the Heavenly Father would grant us wisdom in what to say and when to say it. It would be a while before we were faced with the question, but we would need wisdom when the time came.

That journey was a very special time for me. Mary, Jesus, and I were together every moment. I wasn't away working. I was able to enjoy my wife and "our" son. Our delight was always mixed with wonder – and I knew I would never have a time quite like this with the two of them again.

When the angel of the Lord redirected us to Egypt after Jesus was born, I sent word to Clopas to let him know where we were headed and that we would be delayed returning to Nazareth. At the time, I couldn't tell him when we would be able to return from Egypt, because I had no idea.

I also had no way to send Clopas a message while we were in Alexandria, and he had no way to reach us. So, we prayed all was well with Eli, as well as Clopas and his family. Mary and I talked about the possibilities of what we would be returning to when we arrived home. We prayed that Eli had regained his full strength and hadn't missed us too much – particularly his grandson, whom he had yet to meet.

As we got close to home, Mary said, "And now we have news for him of another grandchild! I am certain he will be overjoyed at the news. We will have to enlarge the house!"

"Oh yes!" I replied. "Happy is the man whose quiver is full of children!"

～

23

UNEXPECTED SURPRISES IN NAZARETH

~

*A*s we entered Nazareth, it looked much the same as it had when we left over two years earlier. Well, almost the same. To my surprise, the first person I saw standing outside Eli's home was Clopas! What was he doing here? We saw each other at the same time. I heard him call out for his wife, Mary, and their son, James, as we all began to scurry toward one another.

"Brother, it is so good to see you! We have missed you!" I exclaimed as we embraced.

"It is wonderful to see you all as well, brother!" Clopas replied. "And who is this good-looking young man? Surely this isn't Jesus! He isn't a baby anymore!"

Both Marys quickly joined us, and we all savored our joyful reunion. They had last seen my Mary the afternoon before Jesus was born, and I had last seen Clopas one day later. Much had happened since then. And yes, Jesus had grown, but so had their son James. He had just turned nine years old.

. . .

We all had so many questions, and there was much news we needed to catch up on. "This is an unexpected blessing," I exclaimed. "We never expected to see you here in Nazareth. What brings you here?"

Clopas paused and looked at his wife before answering. Out of the corner of my eye, I saw my Mary anxiously looking for her father. But she remained there by my side so she could hear Clopas's news.

"Brother, when I last saw you," Clopas began, "you asked us to travel back home through Nazareth so we could check on Eli. I promised you we would. As we began our journey home, Mary and I talked about the way the two of you were being treated by Achim and his family and by your neighbors. We decided we needed to move here to Nazareth to help you and encourage you. There was really nothing to keep us in Cana any longer. We knew it was what God would have us do.

"When we arrived in Nazareth, Eli was disheartened you two would be delayed in your return, but he rejoiced in the news of Jesus's birth. Jesus, Your grandfather was absolutely delighted to hear about you! He also seemed genuinely pleased about our decision to move to Nazareth. We quickly realized we were not moving here solely to encourage you when you returned, we would also be encouraging Eli in your absence.

"I traveled to Cana while Mary and James remained here in Nazareth. I settled our affairs, gathered our few belongings, and brought them back here. While we waited for you to return, we stayed in your home.

"Two months later, we received your message that an angel of the Lord had directed you to go to Egypt. You had asked that we continue to care for Eli, but you obviously did not know of our decision to permanently move here. We marveled at the goodness of God as He ordered all our steps!"

Then Clopas hesitated for a moment before continuing. "Mary, I am sorry to tell you your father never fully recovered from his fever. As time went on, his health continued to decline, and within a few months he died. On the day before he took his last breath, he told me how grateful he was to God for all of His many blessings. He told me God had given him a wife whom he had loved with all his heart."

Mary began to weep. I held her in my arms while Clopas continued. "He told me, 'God has given me a special daughter whom He has honored above all other women. She is my pride and treasure, shining brighter than all others. He has given me a son-in-law who is not only a good son but also a good friend and a righteous man. And most of all, God has allowed me to be the grandfather to His Son – the Messiah – whom I will not meet now, but I will meet one day in heaven!'

"Eli died peacefully with those praises on his lips. He loved you all. And he died knowing he will see you again on the day of resurrection.

"Before he died, he asked me to move my family into his home, to watch over your home, and to keep the family carpentry trade going until your return. I promised him I would do so."

Though Eli's death had taken place over a year before our return, for us it had just occurred. We immediately entered a time of mourning.

∾

24

OUR FAMILY GROWS

~

Those initial days back in Nazareth were difficult. Mary and I both so wished we could have been by Eli's side during his illness and throughout his last days. We grieved his death – but we also grieved that we hadn't been there with him. We knew God had ordered our steps, but it was still hard.

It was gripping to watch Jesus's response through all of this. He had never known His grandfather – at least on this side of heaven – but He saw the pain Eli's death caused Mary and me. He wept with us. One day He told us, "Death was never part of the Father's plan. He, too, grieves the pain and sadness that it causes. But one day soon, death will be defeated. And one day, there will be no more pain and suffering!"

He spoke those words with an authority that surpasses that of anyone I have ever known – and, at the time, Jesus was less than three years of age! Throughout those days, He reminded Mary that Eli was now in a much better place where there are no tears. His words spoke peace and comfort to His mother's heart.

. . .

As the weeks passed, the grief began to lessen. We began to settle back into life in Nazareth. Clopas and I decided to partner in the carpentry trade. It was just like our younger days when we worked together in Cana. He had done a good job of maintaining the trade in my absence, and it felt right to be working together again.

We also noticed our neighbors had become more accepting of us. Perhaps it was because people were drawn to Jesus. Everyone stopped to look at and talk to this charismatic little boy. People admired how mature He was for His age but also how He brightened every heart wherever He went.

We would still on occasion see a neighbor whispering behind our backs, but the open persecution we had experienced before Jesus was born seemed to have passed. Mary and I also decided it had something to do with our grief over Eli's death. The town had truly tried to minister to our sorrow – even Rabbi Jacob.

One day while Clopas and I were working on a job, James came running to tell me Mary was in labor. I needed to get home right away. When I arrived, my sister-in-law and the town midwife were both with Mary. Though I tried to convince them I was experienced in helping Mary give birth, neither one of them would hear a word of it. They both told me to wait outside with the other men!

Clopas, James, and I all nervously waited. Jesus, on the other hand, assured us everything would be fine. He reminded me that the pain of childbirth wasn't a part of the Father's original plan, either. It never ceased to amaze me to hear a three-year-old say things like that! It wasn't long before I heard the startled cry of a newborn baby and the announcement from my sister-in-law, "You have a son!"

Jesus and I entered the room to see the newest addition to our family. There weren't any animals in the room looking on, and the baby's bed had never been used as a feeding trough. Otherwise, Mary seemed as contented holding him in her arms as she had been when she first held Jesus. It was a reminder that all life is a precious gift from God!

.   .   .

Clopas and James soon joined us. Clopas asked, "What name will you give him?"

Mary looked at our nephew and replied, "James, if it is OK with you, we are going to call your new cousin James as well! The name means 'one who follows' and it is our prayer he will follow God every day of his life. So, the two of you will share that important name!"

My nephew looked quite pleased with the answer. Jesus looked at His baby brother and smiled. He had always been a Son, but He had never been a brother. He was going to enjoy this! I saw Him looking into James's eyes. He was looking into his very soul – and I knew He could see James and all he would ever become.

It was a precious night for our family. A family of three had now become four, and something told me we weren't finished.

~

25

OUR FAMILY GROWS EVEN MORE

❧

*A*s the years passed, our family did continue to grow. Two years after James was born, God gave us another son. We named him Joseph. He would be my namesake and a continuing reminder of God's faithfulness.

One year later, God blessed us with Jude, which means "praise." He was to be a constant reminder to us of the great praise that is due to our God and His faithfulness. I had once prayed earnestly for a son, and now God was granting my heart's desire – exceeding, abundantly beyond my greatest hope. One year after that came Simon. Jesus now had four younger brothers – and I had five sons!

Jesus was seven years old when Simon was born. He was already a great help to Mary and me. He was a natural craftsman. I began to teach Him how to use my tools when He was four years old. Very soon, He was fashioning woodcarvings that surpassed the work of many seasoned carpenters.

. . .

As a matter of fact, when He was six years old, He carved a set of animals for James, together with a small wooden ark. I was amazed by the intricate detail, even on animals Jesus had never seen – at least on this side of heaven.

But then I remembered: He knew exactly what each of those animals looked like. He had been with His Heavenly Father when they were created. His handiwork and craftsmanship were already on display in them and through them.

When Jesus gave James the set of animals and the ark, He repeatedly told James the story of Noah and the flood until James knew the story by heart. He taught James the meaning of a rainbow and the fact that Jehovah God keeps every promise!

When James was a little older, Jesus made dolls for him representing David and Goliath. They became two of his most prized possessions as he repeated the story Jesus taught him about how our ancestor, King David, defeated the Philistine giant. He reminded James that God would give him the strength and ability to accomplish everything He set before him.

After Simon was born, Mary told me to stop praying for sons and to start praying for daughters! Those prayers were answered with the birth of little Mary two years later and Salome one year after that. We chose the name Salome in honor of the young girl who had been a friend to Mary when she was pregnant with Jesus. She had continued to be her friend as the years passed.

We were now a family of nine! Each time our family grew, so did our humble home. We added a little space here and there. The five boys slept in one slightly enlarged room. The girls had a much smaller room. And Mary and I had a small room for ourselves.

Jesus was a good big brother to them all, and they all looked up to Him. But He and James, as the two oldest, enjoyed a special bond.

· · ·

Because of their unique relationship, I have asked James to help me tell parts of the rest of my story.

"Jesus helped our parents teach each of us children to be a servant to the others," James said, "and to always think of others in a selfless and loving way. But He didn't just say it in words; He lived it out and modeled it in all He did. I wanted to be just like Him!

"But, no matter how hard I tried, I wasn't able to be just like Him. Jesus never disobeyed our parents. He never did anything to any of us children out of spite or envy. He never got angry or wanted His own way. And when I say never, I mean never!

"It was as if He couldn't sin! I think I started to notice it when I was five. I realized my parents never needed to punish Him for doing something wrong. And it wasn't just that He didn't do anything wrong – He didn't seem to *want* to do anything wrong!

"Our parents taught us we were to care for all of our brothers and sisters – but we were particularly to care for the sibling immediately younger than ourselves. Jesus was to watch out for me, I was to watch out for Joseph, Joseph for Jude, and so on. We were to teach our younger sibling what we had learned. And we were to stick with it until the younger sibling had grasped the skill or the teaching.

"Jesus never got frustrated with me, but I got frustrated with Joseph all the time! Jesus never raised His voice to me, but I would sometimes become so impatient with Joseph I would raise my voice and say things in a mean way. Why couldn't I be more like Jesus?"

~

26

A TRIP TO JERUSALEM

≈

*M*ary and I had not yet told the other children Jesus was the Son of God. We had not felt God leading us to do so. But James, unlike the rest of his siblings, was starting to question why Jesus was so different in His attitudes and actions.

Soon after James turned nine, he and Jesus began to compete with each other athletically. Whenever they were not helping me with my carpentry work or doing their studies, they were often playing together with a ball they had fashioned out of an animal skin stuffed with husks.

"Jesus and I enjoyed kicking the ball back and forth to each other," James recalls, "and we created a game in which we assigned scores for the farthest or most difficult kicks. As we grew older, so did the complexity of our game.

"Jesus was always stronger than I was. We tested our strength by lifting stones. We used heavy round stones of varying weights and challenged each other whether we could lift them to our knees, our waists, our shoulders, or above our heads. Though Jesus always outlifted me, I learned early on I was faster than He was. We were often seen running throughout the Galilean hills.

"I wasn't very old when I learned Jesus's greatest passion was reading and studying the Scriptures. Early in the morning and after the end of the workday, Jesus could often be found at the synagogue reading the Scriptures, listening to teachings, and discussing truths with the rabbis. He instilled within me, as well as all our brothers, a thirst for the Scriptures. This was particularly true of our younger brother, Jude."

When Jesus was twelve, Mary, the children, and I traveled to Jerusalem for the celebration of Passover. Clopas and his family, together with our family, and a number of other families from our town, all traveled together. Those periodic trips to Jerusalem to observe our various religious feasts became a much-anticipated break from everyone's daily routine. The trips were a great opportunity for good fellowship and fun.

The men and women each traveled in separate groups. The younger children and older girls all traveled with the women. Jesus was now old enough to travel with the older boys in their group. It was possible to go for days without seeing an older son because he was off with the others.

The day after we arrived in Jerusalem, our family went to the temple to offer our sacrifice to the Lord. As we continued to pray, Mary and our daughters went to the court of women, and the boys and I went to the men's court.

"After a while, I saw Jesus walk over to the area where the rabbis were teaching," James remembers. "He sat down and joined them. I soon walked over to sit with Him. Before long, He was participating in the conversation – asking questions, giving answers, and quoting Scriptures. I couldn't imagine myself speaking up like that, at my age or His. And apparently some of the men were questioning His right to speak. But soon His knowledge of the Scriptures silenced even His most outspoken critics. My brother always amazed me!

. . .

"We remained in Jerusalem for a few more days – and each day Jesus slipped off to the temple to engage in conversation. My father allowed me to join Him twice more. Each time, I noticed that more people were coming just to see the young boy who was speaking with an authority that challenged – or even overshadowed – that of the religious leaders."

The next day, we departed for home. That evening Mary began to ask if anyone knew where Jesus was. He had walked with the older boys on our way to Jerusalem, so we believed He was doing so on our return trip, as well. But soon we discovered that none of the older boys had seen Him.

This was unusual for Jesus. He had never done anything close to disobeying Mary or me! We couldn't imagine what had happened to Him. Mary and I were worried and decided to return to Jerusalem to find Him. Clopas volunteered to join us in our search.

I told the rest of the family to continue the journey home under the charge of my sister-in-law. I instructed James to help his aunt watch out for the rest of his brothers and sisters. I could tell he was proud to be given the responsibility of being the "older" brother!

For three days we searched for Jesus all over the city. But on the fourth, we decided to go to the temple. There we found Jesus sitting among the rabbis discussing the Scriptures. When we saw Him, His back was to us. But we saw the look of astonishment on the faces of those sitting around Him. He spoke in a way that amazed them – and not just because He was so young!

～

27

THE FATHER'S BUSINESS

~

*M*ary, Clopas, and I watched for a short while before Mary spoke up. *"Why have You done this to us? Your father and I have been frantic searching for You everywhere."* [9]

Jesus stood up and looked at her with compassion. He saw the concern on all our faces. But what He said next would forever alter the way we saw Him. He answered, *"Why did you need to search? You should have known that I would be in My Father's house."* [10]

He had not spoken those words disrespectfully. He would never do anything to dishonor His mother or His father – including His earthly father. But He knew He always needed to honor His Heavenly Father and in so doing, He would truly be honoring us all. He needed us to understand that truth.

We all thought about what He said as we made our way home to Nazareth. It was obvious there would still be times we needed to adjust our plans to align with those of the Father. Mary and I had done so in the days leading up to and following His birth, and we would need to continue to do so as He grew through adolescence into adulthood.

We realized the time had come to tell the other children about their brother. Though the younger children would not fully understand everything, we knew it would be best if they all heard the news at the same time. We began by telling them Jesus had stayed in Jerusalem after we left to be in His Father's house and about His Father's business. You can imagine their quizzical expressions.

So, we told them Jesus's story from the beginning while He sat beside us, listening intently but never once trying to interject. He knew His siblings needed to know who He was – but He was still their older brother and did not want that relationship to change. Joseph and Jude received the news with some of the same questions James had. As expected, the others were too young to really grasp what we were telling them.

I have asked James to share how the children responded to the news.

"Our father and mother told us the story of how Jesus had come to be born," James recalls. "They explained that though my father was Jesus's earthly father, Jesus is in fact the Son of God. For all my life, I had known Him as my big brother. Now I was being told He was God's Son.

"A lot of things made more sense after that revelation. His teaching and understanding of Scriptures for one, and His sinless behavior for another. But it also caused me to look at Him much differently – and somehow, I knew our relationship would never be quite the same.

"I am ashamed to admit I secretly became jealous of Jesus. How could I ever measure up to a brother who is the Son of God? I was certain I would always be seen as inferior in the eyes of my mother and father. No angels had announced my birth! And no wise men from distant lands brought gifts to herald my arrival!

. . .

"As jealousy began to take root in my heart, so did anger and bitterness. If Jesus was the Son of God, why did we live in such humble surroundings? Why didn't we live in a palace, lavished with the riches of this world? Why does our father have to work so hard to earn a living to provide for us?

"It wasn't Jesus who changed that day, it was me. He never once – before or after – lorded over me as my older brother, let alone as the Son of God. I knew He loved me. He was always humble and gracious. He always treated me with compassion and concern. He always looked out for my best. None of that ever changed."

As the weeks and months passed, the children still had occasional questions, but for the most part life continued on as normal. We still worked hard together. The boys still played hard together. We had many good times together as a family.

Jesus taught his younger brothers how to swim, how to carve like craftsmen, and how to play ball. He made dolls for his sisters and was ever their protective big brother. He taught them all how to honor their parents, how to study the Scriptures, and how to treat one another with love and respect.

Mary and I were always careful not to say, "Why can't you be more like Jesus?" But we knew the children – particularly the older boys – still placed that pressure on themselves.

Mary and I viewed all of the children as gifts from God. But even we had to confess to each other that though we loved all of the children equally … we couldn't help but *marvel* at Jesus.

∽

28

A FALL THROUGH THE ROOF

~

*N*azareth was continuing to grow, so there was no shortage of work for Clopas, our sons, and me. Jesus, now twenty years old, had achieved the distinction of being a master carpenter. In many ways, He had exceeded His uncle and me a long time ago. Many of those wanting to hire us to do carpentry work were now asking for Him specifically.

Few people in our community remembered the story of Jesus's miraculous birth. Rabbi Jacob had long ago died. Many of our neighbors had died or moved away. A handful of people still whispered behind our backs – but their whispers were about the illegitimacy of His conception, not His deity. The town viewed Him as the oldest of my five sons.

Friends and neighbors often commented about how proud Mary and I must be of the man Jesus had become. Each time they did, I saw James grimace a little, but his reaction had more to do with his state of mind than it did with the comments. On the job, however, all my sons took their lead from Jesus, because they knew He was now the master carpenter.

· · ·

A few days ago, we were making repairs to the roof of the synagogue. Parts of the roof had begun to deteriorate and leak. It was a fairly routine job. I had performed roof repairs most of my life. But that day I stepped onto a section of the roof I thought was sound – only to discover it was not. Down I fell through the roof.

I landed on the floor two stories below after first hitting a bench. I heard and felt the bones in both of my legs snap just before I struck my head on the floor. I don't remember much after that.

"But I sure do," James recalls. "Jesus called out to Jude, who was already on the ground, to run and get the midwife and find the rabbi. The two of them were the most experienced in our town in providing medical care. Jesus and I quickly climbed down the ladder to tend to our father. We could see his legs were folded beneath him in an unnatural way. Jesus called out to our brother Joseph to go get our mother.

"Jesus looked at our father and assessed his injuries. He cautioned me not to move his legs until the midwife or rabbi had arrived. He tore His shirt, handed me a portion, and told me to use it to apply pressure to the gash in our father's leg, which was bleeding profusely. He did the same to the wound on father's head. As we knelt there beside our father, I knew Jesus was praying.

"It seemed like an eternity before the midwife arrived, followed immediately by the rabbi, and then our mother. Mother took over the task of applying pressure to the wound on father's head. The midwife and rabbi tended to the gash in his leg before carefully straightening both legs. We were all grateful that father was unconscious – otherwise, the pain would have been unbearable.

"While they treated the wound on our father's head, the rabbi told Jesus to craft a stretcher we could use to transport him back home. He and I quickly fabricated a stretcher from materials available there in the synagogue.

• • •

"While we were assembling the stretcher, I looked over at my mother, who was now kneeling beside our father and assisting the rabbi and midwife however she could. Concern was written all over her face. But I noticed something else. She kept looking at Jesus – with expectation."

"'Jesus, please heal him!'" my mother pleaded.

"I thought, 'Of course! Jesus is the Son of God!' Though we have never seen Him perform any miracles, as the Son of God He has the power to do so. Why didn't I think of that? All Jesus needs to do is say the word and our father will be healed! But, why hasn't He thought of that on His own? Why hasn't He already done it? Why did our mother even have to ask Him?

"I looked over at Jesus and nodded my head in agreement, as if to say, 'Yes, Jesus, go ahead and do Your thing. Heal our father!'

"Even amid the jealousy I often felt toward Jesus," James continues, "there was never any doubt in my mind He loved our father with all His heart. I knew He would always do whatever He could to help our father. And as the Son of God, I knew He had the ability to do whatever was needed – even the miraculous!

"At that moment, I became completely overcome with emotion and said, 'Jesus, please go ahead and heal our father!'"

∽

29

"IT'S NOT THE FATHER'S TIME."

❧

*J*ames continues, "The rabbi and midwife looked at both my mother and me curiously. It was obvious they were surprised we were asking Jesus to heal our father. They knew He was an experienced carpenter, but those skills wouldn't help Him now. My father needed medical care, and they were the ones with that ability.

"They assured my mother and me they were doing all that was humanly possible. But they looked even more puzzled when Jesus said, 'It is not yet the Father's time. Very truly I tell you, the Son can do nothing by Himself. He can do only what He sees His Father doing, because whatever the Father does, the Son also does.'

"Jesus didn't say He *couldn't* heal our father; He said He *wouldn't* heal our father –because it wasn't the right time! How could it not be the right time? That didn't make any sense! If He's the Son of God, He can do anything He wants to do! I could feel myself getting angrier and angrier.

"I looked at my mother. Though there was a deep sadness in her eyes, she responded to Jesus's words with a slow nod as if she understood. I turned back toward Jesus. Though I could see it pained Him to not help our father, His expression gave me no consolation. I began to seethe.

"But at that moment, father began to groan. He was starting to wake up. The rabbi and midwife had successfully stopped his bleeding, but now they had turned their attention to setting his broken bones. They asked Jesus and me to gently place the stretcher underneath his body. We all worked together to get it under him while moving his body ever so slightly.

"Jesus then cut lengths of wood to be used as splints. Mother tore pieces of her cloak to be used as ties for the splints. I helped wrap the ties around each leg to hold the splints in place after the rabbi and midwife set the bones.

"Once the splints were in place, Jesus and I carefully picked up the stretcher and began to carry him home. By now, my brother Joseph had alerted our remaining siblings and they accompanied us."

While Jesus and James were carrying me home on the stretcher, I became fully awake. Every part of my body hurt, and every now and again the slightest movement would cause a sharp jab of pain. The trip seemed to last forever, but we eventually made it home. Slowly, they set my stretcher down on the bed.

The rabbi told them to leave the stretcher underneath me. There was no need to move it just yet. I apologized to them all for doing something so stupid as falling through a roof!

I could see they were all worried, so I decided to lighten the mood of the moment when I grinned at them all and said, "Let this serve as a reminder to all of you men to always be careful where you step on a roof!"

The midwife told me I would be confined to my bed for several weeks to allow the bones in my legs to heal, and it would be many months before I would be able to return to my work. In the meantime, Jesus, my other sons, Clopas, and his sons would take care of the business; Mary and my daughters would nurse me back to health. I was mindful of how much worse things could have been and how much Jehovah God has blessed me with my family.

Over the years, Mary and I had learned that the best opportunity for the two of us to talk was after the rest of the family was asleep. Tonight was no exception. I could tell something was bothering her as she went about making sure I was as comfortable as possible.

"I asked Jesus to heal you today," she said quietly.

"How did He respond?" I replied.

"He told me it wasn't yet the Father's time."

I could see His answer was bothering her, so I asked, "What did you think when He said that?"

She looked down before replying. "I felt betrayed – by my son and by my Heavenly Father. I know Jesus can heal you. I know the Creator and Giver of Life is able to mend your body. For over twenty years God has asked us to adjust our lives in order to give birth to His Son and raise Him from infancy. I've never asked anything in return until today. But still, His answer was 'no!'"

Mary had never expressed a word of doubt about Jesus from the day of the angel's announcement until now. She had always been my pillar of faith. Now it was my opportunity to be hers. "Mary," I said, "His answer wasn't 'no.' His answer was 'not yet.' In human terms, Jesus has always been a faithful son to us, and in every way, God has always been faithful to us – and He always will be. His ways are not our ways. His thoughts are not our thoughts.

. . .

"The Father set His plan in motion long ago for His Son to come to this earth. His purpose is so much bigger than my few broken bones. It is not for Him to adjust His plan based upon what is happening in our lives; it is for us to adjust our lives to Him!"

∾

"UNTIL THAT DAY!"

~

*J*ames picks back up telling the story.

"Early the next morning, my mother discovered my father was burning up with fever. We called for the midwife and the rabbi. When they arrived, they told us an infection had set in. They prepared a poultice of roots and herbs to treat the infection. My mother and sisters continued to place cold compresses on his brow and arms to bring down the fever. Several hours passed, but nothing seemed to be helping.

"All of us were gathered there with him. Uncle Clopas and his family were there, as well. The last to arrive in the room was Jesus. It was only then I learned He had spent the night in the garden outside of the village. I knew He often went there to pray. Apparently, He had been up all night praying for our father.

"The rabbi told us it wouldn't be long now. The infection had spread throughout my father's body. It was all we could do to hold back our tears.

I found myself staring at Jesus. Everything within me was demanding to know why He wouldn't heal our father! It was at that moment I saw father open his eyes."

As I looked up at James and the others, I knew God was giving me one last moment with my family. I turned my head and looked at little Salome. I spoke a word of blessing over her. Then I continued to do the same over each one of my children from the youngest to the oldest, concluding with James.

Then I said these words: "Jehovah God has blessed me with a wife who loves Him with all her heart – and loves me with that same heart. For many years I cried out to Him for sons and daughters – and He graciously blessed me with each of you. Clopas, you have stood by my side all your life, and you have never wavered in your trust and support. Each one of you has been an expression of the Father's love for me.

"Jesus, Jehovah God has permitted me to be Your father, as well, and has ordered all our steps for You to be Mary's and my son here on earth – and for all these gathered around this bed to be Your family. I do not know what the Heavenly Father has in store for You while You remain on this earth, but as Your mother's oldest son, I ask you to care for her and all Your family when I am gone.

"And family, I charge you to honor Him and respect Him as your older brother. Jehovah God has given you a great privilege – to know His Son as brother and as Messiah. God will reveal who He is when the time is right. Jesus will follow the Father's timing, and you must trust Him to do so. Some of you have asked why Jesus has not healed me. I say to you simply because it hasn't been the Father's time.

"Trust the Father and trust His Son – even more than you have trusted me. For I am simply a fallible man like each of you, but Jesus and the Father are infallible. They deserve your trust because they are worthy of your trust."

. . .

I'll leave it to James to tell you what happened next.

James recalls, "Jesus looked at our father then turned to look at the rest of us. He told us the time was quickly drawing near for our father to step from this life into paradise. He reminded us that in paradise there is no pain, there is no suffering, and there are no tears. He told us it is a place beyond anything we can imagine that the Heavenly Father has prepared for those who love Him and are looking ahead by faith to the redemption of their sins.

"He told us that if we had seen it – like He has – we would never want to stand in our father's way of entering into it. And He said one day very soon, He will lead our father and the host of others who are gathered in paradise into the presence of the Heavenly Father – according to the Father's timing.

"Then Jesus reached down, wrapped His arms around our father, kissed him on the cheek, and said, 'Father, until that day.'

"With his last breath, our father smiled and looked directly into Jesus's eyes as he said ... 'Until that day!'"

~

PLEASE HELP ME BY LEAVING A REVIEW!

i would be very grateful if you would leave a review of this book. Your feedback will be helpful to me in my future writing endeavors and will also assist others as they consider picking up a copy of the book.

To leave a review:
    Go to: amazon.com/dp/B09F5QW1B2
    Or scan this QR code using your camera on your smartphone:

Thanks for your help!

~

COMING SOON

... the next books in "The Called" series

Experience the stories of these ordinary men and women who were called by God to be used in extraordinary ways through this series of first-person biblical fiction novellas.

Book #2

Coming February 18, 2022

A Prophet Called Isaiah

Raised in the king's palace, no other prophet had his unique perspective to counsel kings and foretell the coming of the One who is the King of Kings.

Available to order at amazon.com/dp/B09F595H7G or scan this QR code using your camera on your smartphone.

Book #3

Coming May 20, 2022

A Teacher Called Nicodemus

In a day when most religious leaders were known for their efforts to discredit the ministry of Jesus, there came one who earnestly sought Him.

Available to order at amazon.com/dp/B09K3KJDW2 or scan this QR code using your camera on your smartphone.

THE EYEWITNESSES COLLECTION

... you will also want to read "The Eyewitnesses" Collection

These four books of short stories chronicle the first person eyewitness accounts of eighty-five men, women and children and their unique relationships with Jesus. You'll hear from some of the characters you met in *"A Carpenter Called Joseph"* and learn more about their stories.

Little Did We Know – the advent of Jesus (Book 1)

Not Too Little To Know – the advent – ages 8 thru adult (Book 2)

The One Who Stood Before Us – the ministry and passion of Jesus (Book 3)

The Little Ones Who Came – the ministry and passion – ages 8 thru adult (Book 4)

Available through Amazon.

THROUGH THE EYES SERIES

... the other books in the *"THROUGH THE EYES"* SERIES

Experience the truths of Scripture as these stories unfold through the lives and eyes of a shepherd, a spy and a prisoner. Rooted in biblical truth, these fictional novels will enable you to draw beside the storytellers as they worship the Baby in the manger, the Son who took up the cross, the Savior who conquered the grave, the Deliverer who parted the sea and the Eternal God who has always had a mission.

Through the Eyes of a Shepherd (Book 1)

Through the Eyes of a Spy (Book 2)

Through the Eyes of a Prisoner (Book 3)

Available through Amazon.

LESSONS LEARNED IN THE WILDERNESS SERIES

The Lessons Learned In The Wilderness series

A non-fiction series of devotional studies

There are lessons that can only be learned in the wilderness experiences of our lives. As we see throughout the Bible, God is right there leading us each and every step of the way, if we will follow Him. Wherever we are, whatever we are experiencing, He will use it to enable us to experience His Person, witness His power and join Him in His mission.

The Journey Begins (Exodus) – Book 1

The Wandering Years (Numbers and Deuteronomy) – Book 2

Possessing The Promise (Joshua and Judges) – Book 3

Walking With The Master (The Gospels leading up to Palm Sunday) – Book 4

Taking Up The Cross (The Gospels – the passion through ascension) – Book 5

Until He Returns (The Book of Acts) – Book 6

The complete series is also available in two e-book boxsets or two single soft-cover print volumes.

Available through Amazon

For more information, go to:

wildernesslessons.com or kenwinter.org

WildernessLessons

ALSO AVAILABLE AS AN AUDIOBOOK

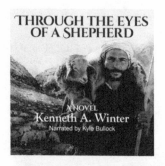

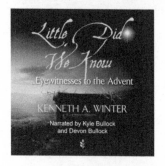

SCRIPTURE BIBLIOGRAPHY

～

Much of the storyline of this book is taken from the Gospels according to Matthew and Luke. Certain fictional events or depictions of those events have been added.

Some of the dialogue in this story are direct quotations from Scripture. Here are the specific references for those quotations:

(1) Matthew 2:20-23
(2) Psalm 127:3, 5
(3) Luke 1:46-49, 54-55 (CEV)
(4) Luke 2:10-12
(5) Luke 2:14 (NIV)
(6) Matthew 2:13
(7) Luke 2:29-32 (ESV)
(8) Matthew 2:20
(9) Luke 2:48
(10) Luke 2:49

∾

LISTING OF CHARACTERS
(ALPHABETICAL ORDER)

∼

Many of the characters in this book are real people pulled directly from the pages of Scripture — most notably Jesus! i have not changed any details about a number of those individuals —again, most notably Jesus — except the addition of their interactions with the fictional characters or events. They are noted below as "UN" (unchanged).

In other instances, fictional details have been added to real people to provide backgrounds about their lives where Scripture is silent. The intent is that you understand these were real people, whose lives were full of all of the many details that fill our own lives. They are noted as "FB" (fictional background).

In some instances, we are never told the names of certain individuals in the Bible. In those instances, where i have given them a name as well as a fictional background, they are noted as "FN" (fictional name).

Lastly, a number of the characters are purely fictional, added to convey the fictional elements of these stories . They are noted as "FC" (fictional character).

∼

Abigail – wife of Eli, mother of Mary (FC)
Achim – cousin of Joseph, living in Bethlehem (FC)
Alim – an Egyptian merchant (FC)
Anna – the prophetess in the temple (FB)
Annas – a scribe and advisor to Herod who later became high priest (FB)
Ashriel – great grandson of Simeon (FC)
Balthazar – the Babylonian scholar and prince (FC)
Caesar Augustus – Emperor of Rome (UN)
Clopas – brother of Joseph (FB)
Eli – father of Mary (FB)
Eliezer – son of Achim (FC)
Elizabeth – cousin of Mary, wife of Zechariah, mother of the baptizer (UN)
Gabriel – angel of the Lord (UN)
Herod the Great – the tetrarch (FB)
Jacob – rabbi in Nazareth (FC)
James – son of Joseph and Mary, half-brother of Jesus (FB)
James (the less) – son of Clopas and his wife, Mary (FB)
Jesus – the Son of God (UN)
Joseph – son of Jacob, husband of Mary, earthly father of Jesus (FB)
Joseph – son of Joseph and Mary, half-brother of Jesus (FB)
Jude – son of Joseph and Mary, half-brother of Jesus (FB)
Khati – son of Alim (FC)
Levi – a rabbi in Bethlehem (FC)
Mary – mother of the incarnate Jesus (FB)
Mary – wife of Clopas (FB)
Mary – daughter of Joseph and Mary, half-sister of Jesus (FN)
Miriam – wife of Achim (FC)
Moshe – a shepherd in Bethlehem (FC)
Nena – wife of Alim, mother of Khati (FC)
Rebekah – first wife of Joseph (FC)
Salome – young neighbor girl who befriended Mary (FC)
Salome – daughter of Joseph and Mary, half-sister of Jesus (FN)
Sarah – granddaughter of Achim and Miriam (FC)
Shimon – son of Moshe, shepherd boy (FC)
Simeon – the prophet in the temple (FB)
Simon – son of Joseph and Mary, half-brother of Jesus (FB)
Unnamed household manager of Herod's palace (FB)
Unnamed midwife who treated Joseph (FC)
Unnamed rabbi who treated Joseph (FC)
Zechariah – priest, husband of Elizabeth, father of John the Baptizer (UN)

∼

ACKNOWLEDGMENTS

I do not cease to give thanks for you ....
Ephesians 1:16 (ESV)

... my partner in all things, LaVonne,
for choosing to trust God as we follow Him in this faith adventure
together;

... my family,
for your love, support and encouragement;

... Sheryl,
for always helping me tell the story in a better way;

... Scott,
for the way you use your creative abilities to bring glory to God;

... a great group of friends who have read an advance copy of this book,
for all of your help, feedback and encouragement;

... and most importantly,
the One who is truly the Author and Finisher of it all
– our Lord and Savior Jesus Christ!

∽

ABOUT THE AUTHOR

Ken Winter is a follower of Jesus, an extremely blessed husband, and a proud father and grandfather – all by the grace of God. His journey with Jesus has led him to serve on the pastoral staffs of two local churches – one in West Palm Beach, Florida and the other in Richmond, Virginia – and as the vice president of mobilization of the IMB, an international missions organization.

You can read Ken's weekly blog posts at kenwinter.blog.

～

And we proclaim Him, admonishing every man and teaching every man with all wisdom, that we may present every man complete in Christ. And for this purpose also I labor, striving according to His power, which mightily works within me.
(Colossians 1:28-29 NASB)

PLEASE JOIN MY READERS' GROUP

Please join my Readers' Group in order to receive updates and information about future releases, etc.

Also, i will send you a free copy of *The Journey Begins* e-book — the first book in the *Lessons Learned In The Wilderness* series. It is yours to keep or share with a friend or family member that you think might benefit from it.

It's completely free to sign up. i value your privacy and will not spam you. Also, you can unsubscribe at any time.

Go to kenwinter.org to subscribe.

Or scan this QR code using your camera on your smartphone:

~

Made in the USA
Coppell, TX
18 November 2021

65961705R00073